OUT OF SIGHT

"Vi," I asked, pressing my ear against the door. "Are you there?"

In lieu of an answer the door was immediately flung open. " 'Ere, be quick, like," she cried out, drawing me inside and bolting the door behind us.

From the agitated state she was in it was immediately apparent to me that this was no game she was playing. The trembling lip, the pale face, and the eyes wide with fear told me that much. "What is it?" I gasped. "What's happened?"

"You didn't see it?" she asked in a horse whisper.

"See it? See what?"

"It's gone then . . . But it could come back," she said with eyes riveted to the door.

"Violet Warner," I announced staring deep into that frightened face, "if you don't tell me this very instant what you're talking about, I shall burst. Now what exactly did you see?"

"A ghost," she blurted out. "That's what."

Other Emma Hudson Mysteries by
Sydney Hosier
from Avon Books

ELEMENTARY, MRS. HUDSON
MURDER, MRS. HUDSON
MOST BAFFLING, MRS. HUDSON

THE GAME'S AFOOT, MRS. HUDSON

SYDNEY HOSIER

AVON BOOKS ◆ NEW YORK

AVON BOOKS, INC.
1350 Avenue of the Americas
New York, New York 10019

Copyright © 1998 by Sydney Hosier
Published by arrangement with the author
Visit our website at **http://www.AvonBooks.com**
Library of Congress Catalog Card Number: 98-92450
ISBN: 0-380-79217-6

First Avon Books Printing: August 1998

AVON TRADEMARK REG. U.S. PAT. OFF. AND IN OTHER COUNTRIES, MARCA REGISTRADA, HECHO EN U.S.A.

Printed in the U.S.A.

WCD   10   9   8   7   6   5   4   3   2   1

Acknowledgments

With special acknowledgment to Nanci Peters, Valerie Hosier, George and Bette Gallagher, George and Charlotte Beier, and Wes Wilson for their continued interest and support.

Contents

ONE

Bound for Brighton

"AH, YES, MRS. Hudson and Mrs. Warner," repeated the man with a broad smile after we had announced ourselves and had the cabbie set our luggage down in front of the registration desk. "We've been expecting you."

"And you, I take it," said I, returning the smile, "would be Mr. Burbage, the gentleman I wrote to in regard to our accommodation."

"Indeed I would be, Mrs. Hudson," he beamed. "Mr. Samuel Burbage, owner, along with my good wife, Dora, of this here lodging house at your service."

Our host was a heavyset man with black pomaded hair slicked down and parted in the middle. And while he did possess a friendly, full-faced countenance, I'm afraid the small beady eyes and the fleshy upturned nose left him with a somewhat comical, piggy-like appearance.

"Now then," he added, "if one of you ladies will just sign here." He extended a pen, which Vi took, and opened up a rather worn guest book. "Come down from Victoria Station then, did you?" he asked conversationally after

1

blotting dry the inked information Violet had set down.

"Yes," I answered. "With the hope that our stay here will be a pleasant one."

"Oh," he readily assured us, "you've no need to worry on that score. Why, after a promenade or two along the boardwalk, taking in the fresh sea air, you'll be hard-pressed to return to London, I'll warrant. Yes, quite the seaside resort, Brighton is, and no mistake. But here, I'd best get your luggage and see you ladies up to your room. No porter here, I'm afraid," he added with a smile. "Just yours truly. Mind you, while it may not be as elegant as the Norfolk or as posh as the Grand, with its one hundred and fifty rooms—which no doubt you saw on your way in—you'll find everything here as clean as a whistle and vittles as nice as ever you had anywhere. If I do say so myself."

"Full up then, are you?" asked Vi.

"We've but two rooms vacant, but then, it's early in the season, ain't it? That's why accommodations are . . . ah—"

"Cheaper," said Vi.

"Less expensive," countered Mr. Burbage, as he struggled to get a hold on our luggage.

"Here," I offered, "let me at least take the portmanteau. It'll help ease your load. Vi, perhaps you can manage the small blue carrying case."

"Don't know why we needed to bring as much as we did, anyway," she said, picking up the case. "Brought enough to clothe a small army, we did."

Ignoring her good-natured grumbling, with which I was all too familiar, we then, as requested by our laden-down host, followed him up a flight of stairs complete with frayed carpeting and none too sturdy bannister. Reaching the top, we made our way along a dreary hallway before at last stopping at the third door down from the landing. "If you'll be so kind, Mrs. Hudson," puffed Mr. Burbage, in between great gasps of air. I took his meaning and turned the knob, pushed open the door, and stepped aside as he staggered into the room, dropping our luggage on the floor with a grateful sigh of relief.

"Here we are then, ladies," he announced with a sweep of his arm as we stepped inside. "Your room. And very nice it is, too, as you can see."

I saw it as nothing out of the ordinary but I, as did Vi, managed a polite smile, acknowledging it as such.

"I should also mention," he continued, "dinner's served between the hours of six and seven o'clock. Cook closes down the kitchen after that though we sometimes manage a sandwich or two for any latecomers."

"Most accommodating of you, I'm sure, Mr. Burbage," said I.

"As for the . . . ah, facilities," he went on, "you'll find it's the third door down the hall to your right."

"The facilities?" queried Vi, knowing full well what the man meant.

Mr. Burbage appeared flustered. "Yes, you know," he stammered, "where you can—that is to say—"

"Oh," she exclaimed, with a wink in my direction in obvious enjoyment of putting the man on, "you mean the loo."

"Yes, right," he acknowledged all too quickly before turning toward the still-open door. "If that's all then," he added, "I'd best be off and let you two ladies get squared away."

"Thank you ever so much, Mr. Burbage," was my parting remark on closing the door behind him, "you've been most helpful."

"It's like they always say, ain't it?" spoke Vi as we each set about hanging up our dresses in a thankfully well-sized closet and placing various other items of apparel in an aged pine dresser. "You gets what you paid for."

"Oh, it's not as bad as all that," I answered. "And the rates *are* quite reasonable."

"Aye, as well they should be, seein' as how, as he says, it's early in the season, like. 'Sides that," she carried on, "we'd need our coats and mufflers, we would, if we ventured out today."

"Well," I countered, "you can't fault the poor man for that."

Actually, if anyone could be faulted I suppose it would have to be none other than myself. I'm afraid the little holiday excursion I had planned had been done a mite too hastily. Not that I regretted coming down to Brighton, mind, but I must admit that with the state of mind I was in at the time, the destination itself mattered less than did the departure. The winter blahs that had given way to spring thaws of heavy rains and wet fog for the better part of April had left me quite out of sorts. Add to that, my seeing to the needs of my illustrious lodgers, Mr. Holmes and Doctor Watson, at all hours of the night and day (being engaged as they were at the time in some such chemical experiment or other) had left me completely exhausted. Though, to give credit where credit is due, Violet did her best in lending a helping hand or two on many an occasion and, knowing I was not in the best of spirits, as it were, my live-in companion did have the foresight to give me wide berth while in the process of tactfully keeping conversation between the two of us down to a minimum.

Unfortunately, or otherwise, things came to a head on the first Sunday in May which had fallen on the anniversary of my beloved William's passing. Having come home from church that morning where I had dabbed a dampened eye and offered up a silent prayer, the remainder of the day found me, as one could imagine, not at my best. And so it was, with supper over and done with, I took myself upstairs to my lodgers' bed-sitting room to collect their dinner trays; for they would, on occasion, have their meals sent up to them rather than take time away from their work. No sooner had I entered the room than I was chided by Doctor Watson for having served up (according to him) a less than tasty meat loaf.

With that, I immediately turned on him and, with tears streaming down my cheeks, gave him quite the tongue-lashing, I did, for what I considered to be rude and uncalled for remarks. For his part, I'm afraid that the poor man was left completely aghast as was the great detective himself; neither of whom, I might add, had ever seen me in such an emotional state. Mr. Holmes sprang up from his chair as did the doctor who, on coming round to me, put his arm about my shoulder in a most consolatory fashion, apologizing as he did and assuring me most profusely that what he had said had been spoken merely in jest.

As for myself, having regained my composure, at least to some degree, I dutifully apologized for my behavior. For I knew that had I been in better spirits I would have realized he'd been having sport with me and, in turn, would have laughed it off with a barb or two of my own at his expense. It was in the hope of extricating myself from both the room and the embarrassing position I now found myself in that I confessed by way of explanation for my outburst that I had not been feeling all that well of late. That being said, I sought to take my leave but the two gentlemen would have none of it. I was promptly ushered into a chair where the good doctor, with a much concerned Mr. Holmes standing to the back of him, proceeded to press, prod, and question me at some length. Having at last satisfied himself, he announced that it was his professional opinion that I was suffering from both a mental and a physical fatigue. Rest and relaxation, I was told, was what I needed. Easy enough for you to say, I thought as he scribbled out a prescription for me, stating as he did in no uncertain terms that I was to have it filled at the chemist's first thing in the morning. I believe it was at that point that I had the idea that a change of scenery might very well be in order.

"Off to Brighton, you say?" questioned Vi, on taking her place at the kitchen table opposite me the following morning. "What's this all about then, eh?"

"Doctor's orders," I smiled.

"What? Doctor Watson? Wants you to go to Brighton, does he?"

"He wants me to get some rest and a change of scenery,'' I answered, adding that Brighton had been my idea before relating to her in some detail the confrontation that had taken place between the doctor and myself the night before.

"Well,'' she replied, on my completing the tale, "if I'd of known that all it takes is an overcooked meat loaf to get a holiday around here, I'd—''

"It wasn't overcooked!'' I snapped.

"Why, Em, it were just a joke, it were,'' she hastened to assure me. "You *do* need a holiday, you do.''

"Sorry, Vi. Yes, I'm afraid I do. And,'' I went on, spreading out the morning paper before me, "I believe I found just the place. I spotted it just before you came in. Look here,'' I added, pointing to a small advertisement in the bottom corner of the page, "where it says 'Brighton— the Burbage House.' ''

"I grant you it sounds nice enough,'' she replied after a scanning of the advert. "But then, you never know, do you?''

"Nevertheless,'' I answered, "I'm sure it'll fit my needs perfectly.''

"But why Brighton?''

"It's no more than an hour and a half by train from London, if that. And besides, I believe the sea air will do me good.''

"Aye, well, quite the place, Brighton is, they tell me. Though I've never been there myself. But they do say there's lots to see and do. 'Course, that's in the summer-time, like.''

"That may be as is,'' I stated, staunchly defending my decision. "But I've no intention of waiting for summer to put in an appearance. I intend to write for accommodation this very morning.''

"Going by yourself then, are you, luv?'' she asked casually enough, though it was perfectly obvious to me what it was she was waiting to hear.

"Why, Violet Warner,'' I smiled, "would I be right in

assuming you'd be willing to keep company with a grumpy old woman like myself?''

"Better that than being left alone here and having to see to the needs of those two up there," was her caustic comment, accompanied by an upward gesture of her thumb. " 'Sides that," she went on, "if you ask me, it's not rest and relaxation you need."

"No? What, then?"

"Why," she replied, as if the answer was there for all to see, "you needs a case to work on, you do. A mystery to solve. That's what you need, luv. We both do, if it comes to that. Murder and mayhem, that's the ticket for getting you back on your feet, and no mistake."

"Somehow," I answered a trifle facetiously, "I never would have thought of murder and mayhem as being a cure-all for a state of mild melancholia. Still," I added, this time not so facetiously, "you could be right. At least to the degree it would help in taking my mind off things other than myself. However, since we've not had for lo these many months one single solitary client come a-calling—Brighton it is."

At but a few minutes to six, we promptly made our way down to the Burbage dining room. Having missed lunch, we all too hastily, I'm afraid, devoured the food placed before us with, if not the best of manners, then certainly with great gusto.

"Enjoyed your meal then, did you, ladies?" queried our host as he sidled over to us between the tables.

"Indeed we did, Mr. Burbage," I replied with a smile. "The sole was excellent."

"Don't know why it is," announced Vi, after a light dabbing of napkin to lips, "but food always seems to taste better when someone else cooks it."

"You know," I chuckled, "you're right. I believe it does. By the way, is this your full complement of guests?" I asked, turning my attention back to our host as I took in the empty tables among those present within the room.

"Why, yes, I should think that it is," he answered. "That's our Mr. Latham over there," he said, indicating a distinguished-looking gentleman of fifty-plus years seated to the left of the fireplace. "And the other two pairs of ladies and gentlemen are the Trefanns and the Christies. That's the Trefanns by the window. Oh, and we do have one other, a Mr. Jones, who's not come down as yet, I see. And of course, yourselves."

"Aye, well, we know who we are," quipped Vi.

"As do I, if you take my meaning," he replied, accompanying his remark with what I can only describe as being a conspiratorial wink. Though why on earth he thought his reply warranted it, I had no idea. He continued to stand there with a silly little grin on that chubby face of his, leaving Vi and me feeling slightly uncomfortable. "Well, Mr. Burbage," I spoke at last, "was there anything else you—?"

"If I might take a seat, ladies?" he asked and, before a reply could be given one way or the other, he drew back a chair and promptly sat himself down. "It's about your place of residence," he stated with another of his annoying winks.

"My residence? I don't understand."

"When your lady friend here, Mrs. Warner, signed the guest book this morning," he began, with a smile somewhat akin to that of a smirk, "I never gave it so much as a second glance. That is, not until later when I spotted it. Fair jumped off the page at me, it did."

Violet and I exchanged puzzled glances. "Mr. Burbage," was my bewildered response, "whatever are you talking about?"

He leaned forward, resting an elbow on the table. "You *are* Mrs. Hudson, right?"

"Yes, of course," I replied somewhat indignantly.

"And you do live at 221B Baker Street, right?"

Oh, Lord, I groaned inwardly, knowing only too well what it was he was leading up to. "Yes, Mr. Burbage," I answered with a resigned sigh, "and Mr. Sherlock Holmes and Doctor John Watson are indeed my lodgers. Is that what you wanted to know?''

''I knew it!'' he exclaimed as his roly-poly face broke into an ever-widening grin. ''Quite the fan of Mr. Holmes, I am, as my Dorie will tell you. That's how I knew about Baker Street and you, Mrs. Hudson. Why,'' he carried on, ''you're famous, you are, being mentioned from time to time as you are in the doctor's articles.''

''Famous? Hardly,'' I smiled. ''Simply a landlady, Mr. Burbage. Simply a landlady.''

'' 'Ere, what's all this 'simply a landlady' business, eh?'' interjected Vi. ''Why,'' she carried on, turning to the man, ''Mrs. Hudson here is quite the detective in her own right, she is. Solved a murder or two, she has, if truth be known. And,'' she added, drawing herself up, ''I've been right there alongside her when she did. We're like a team, you might say.''

Needless to say, Mr. Burbage's initial response was one of surprise, if not outright astonishment. After at last accepting the fact that we had indeed from time to time engaged in the pursuit and apprehension of those who had stepped outside the boundaries of law and order, he pronounced himself most keen to hear of our various escapades. I waved the suggestion aside with the promise of our regaling him with a tale or two at a more convenient time.

''Right you are then,'' he replied, obviously masking his disappointment behind a wan smile. ''But with you two being detectives and all,'' he added, readjusting himself in the chair, ''I must confess I was involved, you might say, with the law myself a few years back.''

Startled by this unexpected admission of his, we said nothing but viewed him somewhat questioningly.

''Now there's no need to be giving me the fish-eye, ladies,'' he hastened to assure us. ''What I meant was, I lent them a helping hand, so to speak.''

''Oh, yes? And in what way, Mr. Burbage?'' I asked, not knowing where his conversation was taking us but nevertheless feeling a need to express my interest in it out of politeness, if nothing else.

"It all happened in this very room, it did," he began, clearly grateful for the opportunity to enlighten us. "About ten or twelve years ago, I should say. Height of the season, it was, with weather as nice as ever you could wish for. And what with it being dinnertime, Mrs. Burbage had her hands full, I can tell you, moving about as she did from table to table serving meals while I kept myself busy as well at the front desk going over our accounts. But here, hold on a minute," he suddenly announced, thereby terminating his story for the moment by picking up our half-full carafe of white wine and extending it in my direction. "Perhaps you ladies would like a refill?"

"Thank you, no," I answered. "I'm fine."

"You can top mine off if you've a mind to," spoke my companion.

"Right you are, Mrs. Warner," smiled Mr. Burbage. "Now then," he said, after complying to her request, "where was I?"

"Going over the accounts."

"Right. So, there I stands adding up last month's bills and whatnot, when the front door opens, only partway, mind, but enough for me to see these two blokes standing there, with the older of the two, his hand resting on the doorknob, talking to two bobbies standing just to the back of him. 'Course, I couldn't hear what they were saying but, quick-like, I knew right away something was up."

"No doubt," said I, straight of face, "by exercising, as you did, your powers of deduction."

"Eh?"

"You saw four men outside your door," I stated, "two of whom were uniformed policemen. Which in itself gave you cause to suspect something was afoot."

"Yes, that's right. That's right," he beamed, looking ever so pleased with himself. "Reckon I could give Sherlock Holmes a run for his money, I could."

"Do go on, Mr. Burbage," I replied, as Vi and I allowed ourselves a smile or two.

"In they came," he continued, "the two of them, leaving the bobbies outside, see, and introducing themselves to me, as they did, as Inspector Grimes and Sergeant Radcliffe. And they ask me, very official-like, if I have a Charlie Allbright staying here. 'We've no one by that name,' I tells them. 'Here,' says the sergeant, taking a photo from his pocket, 'perhaps this might help. Look familiar to you, does he?' he asks. 'Why, that's our Mr. Smith, that is,' I answer. And didn't they look right pleased about that. 'And where,' asks the inspector, 'is your Mr. Smith now?' 'Why,' I tells him, 'he's in the dining room just finishing his meal. Why, what's he done?' 'Seated by himself, is he?' asks the sergeant, ignoring my question. 'Yes, that's right,' I says. 'You can almost see him from here.' What with the two dining room doors being slid back, as they are now, Mrs. Hudson," he informed me, "I could just make out the top of his head amidst the other diners from where I was standing at the desk. So, this here inspector and his sergeant remove their hats—I figures it's so they'll not look out of place like—and each goes in one at a time, in different directions. Circling round the room as they do, until they're in back of him."

"And you remained behind the counter, did you?" I asked, becoming, as I was, quite caught up in his narrative.

"What, and miss out on whatever it was that might happen?" he retorted. "Slipped right in behind them, I did, to let Dorie know what was going on as well. That's when I sees the inspector place his hand on the back of Mr. Smith's shoulder, firm-like, and saying, as he did, 'Come along now, Charlie. We don't want any trouble now, do we? There's a good chap.' Well, this here Charlie gives a bit of a start at first, then shrugs his shoulders, knowing that the game is up, and, with nary a word, rises to his feet. With Grimes to the front of him and this here Sergeant Radcliffe to the back of him, they escort him out of the room without so much as an eyebrow being raised by his fellow diners. It was that quick and smooth-like.''

"Very professional from the sound of it," I remarked, before questioning him as to what happened next.

"Once they had him out here in the lobby," he answered, "the sergeant gave him a good searching up and down, like.''

"Frisking, they calls it," announced Vi. "Ain't that right, Em?''

"Mmmm, yes, I believe I've heard it expressed as such," I answered. "But do go on, Mr. Burbage," I urged.

"After the sergeant finishes, as you say, frisking him," he continued, "he's handed over to the two coppers who whisk him away."

"And the inspector and the sergeant—?"

" 'We'll need to make a search of his room,' they tell me," he answered. " 'What for?' I ask. 'Police business,' says the inspector. I suppose then and there I could have asked if they had some sort of search warrant or other," he said. "But ol' Sam Burbage knows it pays to cooperate with the police. 'Sides," he added, "I didn't want 'em to think I had anything to hide or was, as you might say, in cahoots with this Smith bloke.''

"Very wise of you, I'm sure," I answered.

"So," he carried on, "up the stairs we go. I unlocks Smith's door for them and, when I try to follow them in, I'm told to wait outside. But the inspector tells me I can leave the door open if I like. And, oh, didn't they make a mess of things," he groaned in the remembrance of it.

"How d'you mean, a mess?" questioned Vi.

"Why," he answered, "by dumping out drawers, by sheets being pulled off the bed and the mattress turned over, clothes thrown out of the closet as well as scattering the contents of the man's one piece of luggage out onto the floor."

"My heavens!" I exclaimed. "It sounds more like a rampage they were on instead of a search."

"Rampage," he repeated. "That's as good a word as any

to describe it, Mrs. Hudson, and no mistake. 'Here,' I calls out to them from the doorway, 'who's going to clean all this up, eh?' But they just let on like they never heard me.''

"Well, did they find what they were looking for, or what?" quizzed Vi.

"I heard the sergeant call out, 'Over here, Inspector. Take a look at this.' But," he added, "what it was, I dunno. But weren't they grinning from ear to ear when they steps back out into the hall."

"But you never did ask, then, what it was they had come across?" I inquired.

"Ha!" he snorted. "Think they'd tell me if I had? No," he said, "I was more interested in knowing who was going to put the room back in order."

"Left it the way it was, did they?" asked Vi.

"Told me they'd send someone over to put things right," he announced. " 'Course they never did. No need to tell you what Mrs. Burbage thought of it when she saw the mess they made. Fit to be tied, she was. Fit to be tied."

I replied that I could well understand how she would be. "But what," I asked, "had this Smith person done to warrant all this?"

"Never did find out 'til I read about it in the papers," was the disgruntled reply. "Coppers," he huffed, "like I say, never tell you anything, they don't. You'd think," he went on, "what with me solving the case and all, they'd—"

"Solving the case, you say?" interrupted Vi, her voice scarcely concealing her skepticism. "How'd you do that, then?"

"Why," he answered, plainly taken aback that the question should have been asked at all, "as I told you. By my pointing out the man to them. They'd never have caught him if it hadn't been for me, like as not."

"Oh, I see, right," she replied, nodding her head accordingly and adopting a thoughtful countenance while, at the same time, secretly adding a playful tap or two of her shoe to mine from beneath the table.

While I was amused myself by his logic, the fact he had taken it upon himself to balloon his importance out of proportion to the part he played was understandable. It being, no doubt, the most singular event in his otherwise mundane life. "And what exactly," I asked, "was it that you learned from the newspapers?"

"That this here Allbright bloke—or Smith, as I knew him—was some kind of fancy jewel thief."

"A jewel thief!" we chorused. "Pray continue, Mr. Burbage," I urged, with the decision to refill my glass and that of my companion's with the last of the wine.

"The coppers, you see," he began, with an eagerness to continue his tale, "had been on the lookout for him in connection with the theft of some such jewel he'd nicked from the old Windermere estate."

"The Windermere estate? Here in Brighton, is it?" I asked.

"It's just outside the city where all the posh homes are," he informed me, before my adding that, all in all, it must have been quite the exciting time for him. As, no doubt, it would have been for myself had I unknowingly given lodging to some nefarious jewel thief.

"I'd be lying to you if I said it wasn't," he replied. "Headline story it was at the time. Even the London papers picked up on it. In fact," he announced with no little pride, "during the trial, me and the missus were called into court as witnessess, what with him having stayed here and all."

"And Mrs. Burbage," I asked, "what was her reaction to all this?"

"Said all the publicity we received would be bad for business," he answered.

" 'Course, it wasn't," announced Vi. "Not if I know human nature. "Had them lining up for rooms here, like as not."

"Right as rain you are, Mrs. Warner," he gleefully acknowledged. "Told her as much myself at the time. And what was the outcome? Not so much as a single vacancy over the next three seasons. Why," he went on, "we even had people wanting to book into the very room this here Charlie Allbright had stayed in. I'd been right, you see," he added, with his little dark eyes crinkling up in delight.

It was obvious to me as I watched him savor his past moment of glory that this had been one of the few times, if not the first, that he had succeeded in besting his wife by proving her wrong.

"But what I want to know," questioned Vi, harking back to his tale, "is what made the police think he'd be here in the first place?"

Her question never did receive an answer, for at that moment Mrs. Burbage suddenly appeared at our table. Standing before us as she did, her presence (a commanding one at that, I might add) had the effect of curtailing any further conversation on the part of her husband.

Violet and I had met her earlier, of course, for she had shown us to our table, taken our order, and served our meal. As for any interplay of conversation on her part at the time, it remained as sparse as her frame. How unlike her husband she was, I thought. For she was as taciturn as he was gregarious. As narrow as he was wide. As tall as he was short. Gaunt of face with lips razor thin. The only singular similarity between the two being the hair. Like that of her husband it was parted in the middle. Unlike her husband's, it was brought down over the ears and tied into a bun in back.

"Mr. Burbage," said she, addressing her husband in a voice as intimidating as her presence, "we now have new rules, do we, in regard to sitting with our guests during their meals?"

"I just plopped meself down for a minute or two, Dorie," he mumbled, on extricating himself from the chair. "No harm done."

At that point I stepped in to offer up a word or two on his behalf by stating we had no objection to his presence and, indeed, found his conversation most enlightening.

"Yes, yes, Mrs. Hudson," she replied in a most condescending tone, "I'm sure you did. But Mr. Burbage has his duties to attend to, as well he knows."

"I'd best be off then," he announced with a wink in our direction. " 'Fore Dorie here gets the whip out."

"Really, Mr. Burbage!" exclaimed the woman. "I really must apologize for my husband's behavior, ladies," she said, turning to the two of us as her husband ambled off. "The man simply has no sense of decorum."

Vi and I exchanged glances with each other but said nothing, other than my stating to the woman, as we rose to our feet, that I believed Mrs. Warner and I would now return to our room as we each had one or two things ourselves to attend to.

"I don't know about you, Vi," I said, on closing the door to our room behind us, "but I think I'll make an early night of it. This day seemed to go on forever."

"I know what you mean," she replied, stifling a yawn. "And Mrs. Hoity-Toity didn't help things much. What d'you think of her, eh?"

"Mrs. Burbage? A pretentious prig," I answered. "Quite the opposite from her husband, I must say. Here, give me a hand in getting out of this, would you?" I added, turning my back on her.

"Aye, she's that, and no mistake," she agreed, while complying with my request by deftly undoing the first five or six buttons to the back of my dress. "There, she said, "you can get the rest now, can you, luv?"

"Mmmm—yes, thanks."

After a bit of idle chitchat about nothing in particular, we bedded ourselves down on a less than comfortable mattress and eventually drifted off to sleep. How long our journey into the land of Nod lasted, I have no idea. But I do remember Vi waking me up at some point during the wee hours of the morning, in a most agitated fashion, to announce she had heard what she described as odd noises coming from above.

"From above?" I groggily responded. "But there is no room above, is there?"

" 'Ere, how should I know?'' she grumbled. ''But it's keeping me awake, whatever or whoever it is.''

"I'll have a talk with Mrs. Burbage about it first thing in the morning,'' I mumbled, before once more lapsing back into sleep.

TWO

The Captain and Mrs. Warner

WHILE THERE HAD been ample opportunity the following morning to speak to Mrs. Burbage in regard to the odd noises Vi had heard, we had, nevertheless, decided amongst ourselves before coming down to breakfast to let the matter drop. For all I knew, it might have been no more than a bad dream on the part of my companion. Though when I questioned her on that point she was quite adamant (as only Vi could be) in stating otherwise. Still, if true, the question remained, however inconsequential it might have been, just who was it that had lodgings directly over our head? Be that as it may, the thought of accosting the formidable Mrs. Burbage with complaints of hearing bumps in the night was not something either Violet or myself particularly looked forward to. However, we readily assured each other (or at least as convincingly as we could) that should it happen again we would most certainly bring the matter to her attention.

As we settled ourselves down to breakfast we were greeted by the lady herself who, thankfully enough, never did inquire as to whether we had enjoyed a good night's sleep. From his table by the hearth, Mr. Latham offered up a smile and raised his cup in a silent salute of acknowledgement of our presence. As for the Christies and the Trefanns, we garnered from each of their respective tables equally silent and polite nods of the head. How very nice. How very English. I couldn't help but think that I'd rather enjoy a chat with our fellow lodgers should the opportunity present itself. And so it was, with our own breakfast at last over and done with, I finished the remains of my tea and set the cup down feeling that much the better for it.

" 'Least we can't complain about the food," said Vi. "That's one thing in their favor. Not only that," she added as we arose from the table, "but the best part is knowing we don't have to prepare our own meals or clean up afterwards."

"Right you are there," I agreed with a smile. "But it does raise the question as to how Mr. Holmes and the doctor are making out on their own."

"Aye, well, all I can say to that is, I hates to think what your kitchen will look like when we gets back, what with them two muckin' about in it."

"Good morning, ladies," spoke Mr. Burbage on his entering the dining area just as we were on our way out. "Enjoyed your breakfast then, did you?" After assuring the man that we had and, following an added exchange of pleasantries, I asked, in what I hoped was an offhanded way, just who was it that had the room above ours. My question was received with a look of puzzlement.

"The room above? I don't understand," he said. "There is no room above you."

" 'Ere, what's this you're saying?" exclaimed Vi. "No room?"

"Well, no room as such," he explained. "But there *is* an attic."

"An attic," repeated my companion, breaking into a relieved smile. "Oh, well, that's all right then, isn't it?"

"All right?" repeated a thoroughly confused Mr. Burbage. "I'm afraid I don't—Ah, good morning, Mr. Jones," he said, acknowledging a moody-looking, sandy-haired young man who had just entered the room. For his part, Mr. Burbage received no more than a mumbled grunt or two from the man as he passed by. For my part, I couldn't help but think as I watched him cross over to his table and slump down into his chair how utterly forlorn he appeared to be. It was as if he was carrying the worries of the world on those broad shoulders of his. And with our host's attention being momentarily diverted by Mr. Jones as well, Vi and I took that moment to slip back to our room, leaving the master of Burbage House to no doubt ponder over our interest in his attic.

"Well, that's a relief, that is," announced my companion, plunking herself down on the bed. "When he said there were nothing there I thought I was going crackers. What with me hearing noises from above when there weren't no above, if you knows what I mean."

"Mmmm—I daresay it was no more than some creature of the night you heard."

"Creature! 'Ere, what's this you're saying? What kind of creature?"

"Perhaps some owl or bat got into the attic and knocked something over in a panic to get out," I offered up by way of explanation.

"Oh, I see," she huffed. "Owls and bats wearin' boots. Is that it?"

I turned to her questioningly. "Are you now saying that you heard someone clomping about in boots?"

"Well," she hedged, "maybe not boots."

Believing that Vi had let her overactive imagination create a mystery where none existed, I set the subject aside by asking what plans, if any, she had for the rest of the day.

"Plans? Well, I don't know, really," she said. "What with it spittin' rain and all outside, perhaps I'll take myself down to the reading room. They've quite a nice collection of books and magazines from what I saw. How about yourself, luv?"

"I thought I might spend the day catching up on my

correspondence," I answered. "There's a number of letters I've been meaning to write and I suppose now's as good a time as any to get on with it." Which I did. And while the rest of the day proved quiet, relaxing, and uneventful, I can state most unequivocally the same could not be said for the night that followed.

We had taken to our bed at a little after eleven in anticipation of what I hoped would be a good eight hours' sleep. Unfortunately, it was not to be. Sometime during the night I was once again nudged awake by Vi. "What is it? What's the matter? More noises?" I asked, making a halfhearted attempt to raise myself up on one elbow. And as she replied it was nothing like that, I couldn't help but notice the urgency in her voice. "Well, what is it then?" I asked.

"I've got to go to the loo," she confessed in a whisper.

"To the loo? To the loo?" I repeated incredulously. "You mean to say you woke me up at—" I paused and groped at the night table for the little windup clock I had the foresight to bring along and, holding the face of it up to my eyes in the semidarkness of the room, finished my sentence. "—at seventeen minutes after two to tell me that?"

"Well, I can't help what time it is, can I?" she stated defensively.

"Oh, Vi," I groaned, dropping back on my pillow, "if you have to go—go. But why you should think it necessary to wake me to—"

"I thought perhaps you could come along with me, like," she whined. "What with our being in strange surroundings and being late at night as it is."

"For heaven's sake, Mrs. Warner," I retorted, being more than a little annoyed at having my sleep disturbed by what I considered to be a childish and needless request on her part, "it's only just down the hall."

"Oh, I see," she shot back. "And it makes no nevermind to you, does it, if I goes traipsin' off half-naked down there by myself, is that it?"

With a weary sigh I once more raised myself up and, as

calmly as I could, pointed out to her that the wearing of a housecoat over a nightgown would hardly constitute a state of undress. Half-naked, indeed! It was but another fine example of her penchant for overdramatizing a situation. Another example being her hearing noises from the attic—a tale which I had now discredited.

"Right! And thank you very much, I'm sure," she snapped while continuing to show her displeasure with me by making a great to-do of removing herself from the bed.

I lay there listening to her in the darkness as she fumbled about with her housecoat and slippers before at last taking it upon herself to flounce from the room with nary another word spoken between the two of us. Unable to get back to sleep, I waited in a state of drowsiness for her return. And I waited. And I waited. Still no Vi. I turned once more to my clock and, holding it up to a shaft of moonlight, saw the time as being two-thirty. She'd been gone for almost fifteen minutes. She should have been back by this time. Was she playing games? If indeed this was her way of getting back at me, little good it would do her. I could be just as contrary as she. I was to jump out of bed and rush down to see what was keeping her, was I? Not likely. But of course, after waiting no more than a minute or two longer, I did just that. Once out of bed and into my housecoat I opened the door of our room and peered outside. No Vi. It was with feelings of both apprehension and annoyance that I advanced down the darkened hallway until reaching the door of the loo where I paused, listened for a moment or two, then gave it three light taps. "Vi," I asked, pressing my ear against the door, "are you in there?"

"Is that you, Em?" came a voice from within.

"Well, of course it's me," I answered, now more annoyed than apprehensive. "What on earth's been keeping you?"

In lieu of an answer the door was immediately flung open. " 'Ere, be quick, like," she cried out, drawing me inside and bolting the door behind us.

From the agitated state she was in it was immediately

apparent to me that this was no game she was playing. The trembling lip, the pale face, and the eyes wide with fear told me that much. Someone or something had truly frightened her. But what? "What is it?" I gasped. "What's happened?"

"You didn't see it?" she asked in a hoarse whisper.

"See it? See what?"

"It's gone then." Her face broke into a relieved smile, but only for a moment. "But it could come back," she said with eyes riveted to the door. "That's the thing of it, see. That's why I didn't come out."

"Violet Warner," I announced, staring deep into that frightened face, "if you don't tell me this very instant what you're talking about, I shall burst. Now, what exactly did you see?"

"A ghost," she blurted out. "That's what."

"A what!" I heard what she said but couldn't believe my ears.

"A ghost," she repeated, pointing to the door, "out there."

I confess I was caught completely off-guard and, for a moment or two, I didn't know quite how to respond. "Are you saying," I began, very slowly, "that you actually saw a ghost in the hallway?"

"I saw him, all right, and no mistake," she said. "Fair scared me half to death, he did."

"He? This was the spirit of a man you saw?"

"Aye," she acknowledged with an involuntary shudder.

With my companion still visibly upset by her ordeal, I suggested she relax, take a deep breath, and tell me exactly what she saw. She complied to my request and, after regaining a certain degree of composure, began her tale.

"I had just stepped out of the loo," she stated, "what with having made my way down here by myself," she added in a snide reference to our previous set-to, "when I sees this figure of a man walking the hall."

"Coming toward you, was he?"

"No," she said, "walking up the hall away from me, he

was. 'Course I couldn't see him all that good what with that one little gas lamp they've got on the wall. Think they'd have summat better than that, wouldn't you?''

"Yes," I replied, "I thought the same thing myself. But go on," I urged.

"Perhaps you could take a peek outside first," said Vi. "Just to see if he's come back, like."

"If he is a ghost," I answered, as a tiny twinge of skepticism began to take hold, "I'm sure he's got better things to do than wait outside a loo for someone to come out." I knew as soon as I had spoken it was the wrong thing to say.

"What's this?" she snapped back. "*If* he is a ghost? Making it all up then, am I?"

"No, no, not at all," I hastened to assure her. "It's just that there *are* a number of men staying here. Perhaps it was one of them."

"What? The way he was dressed?" She looked me up and down as if I was mad. "Not ruddy likely."

The way he was—dressed? *This* was something new. "Vi, for heaven's sake," I replied, scarcely able to control my exasperation with her, "if you continue to dole out your story in piecemeal fashion we'll be here all night."

"Oh, well, pardon me for living, I must say," came the haughty response. "It's just that certain people always seem to be interrupting, don't they?"

I was too tired to argue. "Do get on with it then," I answered with a weary sigh.

"Right. Well then, like I was saying—what was I saying?"

"You had just come out of the loo," I muttered.

"Right. I'd just stepped outside when I sees this 'ere shadowy figure going up the hall all kinda quiet-like. Gave me a bit of a start at first, he did. Then, like you, I thought he must be one of the gentlemen lodgers or maybe Mr. Burbage. Fact is, I was about to call out, 'Is that you, Mr. Burbage?' That is, until he reached the gaslight and paused, turning a little sideways like, as he did. It were as if he sensed he was being watched. Leastways, that's the impression I got. That's when I sees he's wearing a sea captain's hat and, from what I could make out, shiny brass buttons on his coat. 'Sides that,'' she added, ''he only had one arm.''

"One arm!" I gasped. "Are you sure?"

"Oh, aye," she stated. "I could see one sleeve hanging loose with the bottom of it being tucked into the pocket of his jacket. Thought of old Mr. Findlay right away when I saw it,'' she said, recalling the name of one of our former neighbors who had the misfortune of having to have an arm amputated after falling under the wheels of a runaway carriage. "So there I stood," she continued on, "rooted to the spot, I was. Not sure whether I was seeing things or not. Well, I mean, it all seemed so unreal and all. So I did the only thing I could do."

"Which was—?"

"I closed my eyes."

"You did what?"

"Closed my eyes," she repeated. "I figured if he's still there when I opens them, I'd scream bloody murder."

"And—?"

"And when I did—open them, I mean—he was gone. Vanished, you might say. Like he'd never been there at all. Oh, Em,'' she confided, ''I was ever so scared. All I could think of to do was to get back in the loo, bolt the door, and wait for you to show up. Whatever kept you?''

"I . . . ah, I must have fallen back to sleep for a minute or two," I lied. Better a lie than to admit I believed her absence was due to no more than some childish prank on her part.

How wrong I had been. For not even Vi's vivid imagination could have conjured up a story of having seen some one-armed sea captain looming about the hallway. But a ghost? Then again, why not? While I confess to never having been witness to spectres, celestial beings, or the appearance of a departed loved one, I have never ruled out the possibility of their existence. There have been too many sightings by too many people over too long a time for me to airily dismiss it all as simply nonsense, a hoax, or an aberration of the mind. Indeed, I need look no further than my companion for confirmation of the mysteries that abide twixt earth and sky. I speak of her past ability to engage in out-of-body experiences, which she had shown herself to be adept at on more than one occasion in conjunction with cases we had worked on. To which I confess I had no more rational explanation of it then than I do now. Nevertheless, having said that, the fact that Vi's nightly visitor could also have been someone bent on robbery or, at best, some homeless derelict seeking shelter could not, at this point, be ruled out. Of these thoughts, I said nothing to Violet, being only too well aware of her own opinion as to who and what she had seen.

"There's no one there now," I said, poking my head round the door. With that, we set off at a smart pace down the hall back to our room, being mindful to secure the lock once inside.

"The Burbages will hear about this, and no mistake!" vowed Vi from beneath the covers of the bed. "First thing in the morning, they will." I couldn't have agreed with her more and told her as much myself before at last drifting off into an uneasy sleep. I say *uneasy* for I had awakened at one point with the thought I too now had heard a thumping from above. I put it down as a bad dream and lapsed back into sleep.

It was mid-morning of the next day when Vi and I—seeing Mr. Burbage with his back to us behind the registration desk, sorting through the mail—stepped forward to voice our complaints. "A word or two with you, if we may, Mr. Burbage," I said on our approach.

"If you may?" he echoed, edging himself halfway round with a smile as wide as his girth. "Why, bless you, Mrs. Hudson, I've always time for a word or two. Expecting a letter from Mr. Holmes, are you?" he asked in eager anticipation, while continuing to pigeonhole the various envelopes into their respective slots.

"No, I'm afraid not," I answered, perhaps a little too sharply. Sensing an uneasiness in the air, if not in my manner, he set the remaining envelopes aside and turned full around to question whether anything was wrong.

"Perhaps *wrong* might not be quite the right word to describe it," I replied, with my companion voicing her opinion that *weird* would be more like it.

"Weird?" he repeated. "What's all this about then, eh?"

"I think you should know," I began, "that sometime between the hours of two and three in the morning, Mrs. Warner saw—" I paused. I was about to say *a ghostly figure*, but thought the better of it by announcing she had seen the figure of a man roaming the upstairs hall. "And from her description of him," I continued, "I can assure you it was none of the gentlemen you have currently lodging here. Needless to say, we were both quite alarmed and upset by the incident."

"'Sides that," added Vi, stepping forward, "the night before there were all kinds of funny noises in the attic, like."

Hearing this, I had expected the man to exhibit shock, or at least surprise. On the contrary, his only reaction was to lower his eyes and place his hand up to his mouth. Was he hiding a smile? He was! Not to be taken seriously after having confronted him with the knowledge that there had been some thief or vagrant afoot in his lodgings was simply intolerable. I would have voiced my displeasure in no uncertain words at this effrontery had he not posed a question that took Vi and me completely aback.

"This man you saw, Mrs. Warner," he asked, "he wouldn't have been wearing a sea captain's hat, now would he? And a brass-buttoned coat?"

"Aye!" she exclaimed. "That's right, he was."

"And his right arm," he continued, "did you happen to notice anything—?"

"Gone, it was," she stated. "The sleeve was tucked into the pocket. Remember, Em," she said, turning to me, "I told you as much, I did."

"You know this man then, do you, Mr. Burbage?" I asked, feeling somewhat relieved.

I received a faint flicker of a smile. "In a manner of speaking," he answered. "Oh, Dorie," he called out to his wife on seeing her exiting the reading room, "got a minute, have you?" Dora Burbage paused and scowled. "She hates it when I calls her Dorie, or Dora, far as that goes. Leastways, in front of guests," he confided to us on her approach.

"Then why do you do it if it upsets her so?" I asked.

"One of life's little pleasures," he confessed with a wink and a nudge.

The woman must have sensed something was amiss for, as she joined us at the desk, her first question was to her husband. "Is anything wrong, Mr. Burbage?" she asked.

"It's the ladies here," he announced. "Seems they've seen the captain."

Her hand shot to her mouth—not, as I noted, to cover a hidden smile, but in conjunction with a gasp of obvious astonishment.

"Actually, it was Mrs. Warner who saw him," I announced. "It was late at night, in the hallway, and, well, it gave her a bit of a fright, I'm afraid. The thing of it is," I continued, with misgivings on having brought the matter up in the first place, "if we had known beforehand that the gentleman in question was known to you, I'm sure—"

"Known to me?" she repeated, giving me an odd sort of look.

"Why, yes," I said, now as puzzled as she. "At least that was my understanding."

She whirled on her husband. "You've not told them—is that it?"

"Thought it might be best if you did," he mumbled, avoiding her eyes.

"Right," she said. "Leave it to Mrs. Burbage, like everything else around here. Well then, ladies," she announced with a resigned sigh, "I suppose there's no way to say it than to say it straight out. And that is, by all accounts, what Mrs. Warner saw roaming about the upstairs landing last night was the spirit of a certain Captain John Hammond.''

"A ghost!" exclaimed Vi in a voice that rang through the room. "I knew it! Em 'ere," she added, addressing the Burbages, "wasn't all that sure. But I knew what I'd seen last night, right enough."

"I hadn't discounted the possibility," I replied in a face-saving rejoinder. "In any event," I continued, noting Mrs. Trefann taking in all that she had heard from her stance by the dining room door, "I daresay it won't be too long before it becomes common knowledge among the other guests as well."

"I'll have a word with them," stated Mrs. Burbage, seeing, as did we all, Mrs. Trefann's hasty retreat back into the room. "Mind you," she added, "it's not as if we were trying to keep it a secret, so to speak. Our regulars are well aware of it. Aside from Mr. Latham, those staying here, including yourselves, are all first-time guests."

"That being the case," I said, not to be put off so easily, "you might have made mention of your nightly visitor."

"Yes, but what I'm afraid you ladies don't understand," she carried on as if addressing children, "is that these manifestations do not appear on a regular basis. Is that not so, Mr. Burbage?"

"True enough," he agreed. "Why, it must be a good five years or more since anyone saw the captain."

"Yes, quite right," confirmed his wife. "So you see, there was no reason for either my husband or myself to make mention of it when the knowing of it would merely upset our guests unnecessarily."

"They're really quite harmless, ladies," stated Mr. Burbage. "Why, we wouldn't stay here ourselves if they weren't."

"What's this you're saying?" exclaimed Vi. "*They're* quite harmless? 'Ere, how many you got floatin' around 'ere, eh?"

Mrs. Burbage shot Mr. Burbage a withering glance.

"Two," he mumbled, suddenly looking very uncomfortable. "But," he quickly added, "it's like I say, they're harmless."

"And this other one," I asked, "would be—?"

"His wife," he confessed. "Sarah. Sarah Hammond."

I looked at Vi. She looked at me. Neither of us knowing quite what to say. It was Mrs. Burbage who stepped in to state that if we were entertaining thoughts of cutting short our stay, reimbursements would be made. Though it was her wish, she assured us, that we would stay on as planned. I drew Vi aside to mull it over. Taking into consideration that the chances, according to the Burbages, of ever again encountering the spirit of the captain or, for that matter, his wife as well, would indeed be remote, we informed them of our decision to stay on. That, plus the fact that we'd be able to say we once stayed in a haunted house (everyone's favorite nightmare, is it not?), proved irresistible.

"Oh, Mrs. Hudson," spoke Mrs. Burbage as we were about to take our leave, "there'll be a carriage pulling up outside in a few minutes to take guests down into the main section of the town. It'll give you and Mrs. Warner a chance to do a bit of shopping, if you've a mind. The driver will pick you up in two hours' time to bring you back. I believe the Trefanns are going along as well."

"What do you think, Em?" asked Vi. "Want to go, do you?"

"I think I'll find myself a good book," I answered. "But you go ahead yourself, if you want."

"Aye, perhaps I will. I'll just pop upstairs and get me coat. See you later then, luv."

As she headed upstairs I turned in the direction of the reading room and, on entering, found Mr. Latham hunched forward in an armchair, deeply engrossed in a book. He was a fine figure of a man in his mid-fifties with thinning silver hair and a neatly trimmed moustache. His face, though distinguished, was of a ruddy complexion. No doubt the result of a daily constitutional that consisted of invigorating strolls along the windswept beaches of Brighton.

And, while his attire would find no admirers on London's Saville Row, he nevertheless exhibited the demeanor of a gentleman.

"Mrs. Hudson, good afternoon," he said, raising himself up slightly as I crossed by in front of him. "It *is* Mrs. Hudson, isn't it?" he asked in a voice one would describe as being posh.

"Yes—good afternoon, Mr. . . . ah, Latham?" I questioned, though I knew who he was as I'm sure he knew who I was. Still, it broke an uneasy silence.

"Yes, quite," he answered with a smile.

With our somewhat convoluted introductions over and done with I set about scanning the book-shelved wall for an interesting title. I selected Elizabeth Barrett Brownings *Sonnets from the Portuguese* and settled myself but a chair away from him by the fireplace.

"Have a bent for poetry, do you?" he asked, lowering his book and resting it on his lap.

"Pardon?"

"The *Sonnets*," he replied with an eye toward the cover of my book.

"Oh, yes, I suppose so. Although I *have* read it before, but that was a good many years ago," I confessed.

"Books can be a great source of joy, can they not? Look at them," he continued eyeing the shelved literature. "There they sit, as inanimate as any Egyptian mummy, with but one exception. They can be brought back to life by the simple act of being reread."

"What you say reminds me of a poem," I said, and blurted out the following:

> *Look you now,*
> *How words do march*
> *Across the page*
> *Like some vast army*
> *Now engaged*
> *In freeing tales*
> *That once were told*

> *Round fires bright*
> *By men of old.*
> *So, say I,*
> *Come sit thee down*
> *And read, my friend,*
> *The thoughts that flowed*
> *From mind to pen.*
> *With cover closed*
> *'Tis naught but dead*
> *And only lives*
> *When it is read.*

"Very good. Very good indeed," he remarked when I had finished. "And the author is—?"

"Hudson," I acknowledged demurely, feeling a trifle embarrassed and not a little surprised that I had remembered the words, having set them down—how long ago? I'd forgotten.

"So, the lady detective is also a poet. I *am* impressed."

"Detective—? Ah," I nodded knowingly, "I take it your information comes by way of a certain Mr. Burbage."

"Yes, actually it does," he confessed. "But dash it all, you can't really blame the fellow, can you? I mean, what with all this Sherlock Holmes business you're involved with. I say," he went on, leaning forward and dropping his voice to a whisper, "you haven't come down to Burbage House to solve some sort of mystery, have you?"

"I can thankfully say, Mr. Latham, that I am aware of no such mystery. Are you?" I asked with a touch of bemusement.

"Well, no," he grudgingly replied. "At least, not so far as I know. Unless," he continued, "you count the ethereal wanderings of the good captain and his wife."

"As to that," I answered, "I'm afraid solving the mysteries of the afterlife are above and beyond my earthly abilities."

"But you've see him, have you?" he asked. "The captain, I mean. I caught part of your conversation with the

Burbages," he added by way of explanation. "Mind you, I wasn't eavesdropping, but I couldn't help but—"

"No," I answered, "it wasn't I who saw him but my companion, Mrs. Warner."

"Ah, I see," he responded, sinking thoughtfully back in his chair before inquiring as to whether or not I'd mind telling him exactly what she had seen.

I repeated the story as told to me by Vi, stating that she had also been awakened the night previous by hearing noises emanating from the attic which, however unsettling it was, we could now attribute to ghostly visitations.

When I had finished he sat silently for what seemed the longest time before at last uttering one word: "Strange." Which, in itself, I thought was strange. I was of the opinion that *terrifying, frightening*, or even *fascinating* would have been more apt. "I understand," I said, in a change of subject, "that you stay on here as a regular."

"Yes, true enough," he replied. "Actually, I'm part of the staff, you might say, in that for my lodgings I'm required to help out whenever called upon in regard to maintenance. Our Mr. Burbage, as you may have noticed," he added with a smile in reference to the man's excess weight, "is not in the best physical shape for that sort of thing. I may be somewhat trimmer," he announced with a pat to his stomach, "but still, it doesn't get any easier as the years go by."

I was profoundly shocked by what I had just heard. "Maintenance? You?" I blurted out without thinking. "Oh, I'm sorry," I added just as quickly. "It's just that you don't look—that is to say—"

"Please, don't apologize," he responded with a reassuring smile. "Actually, there's another reason why Mrs. Burbage keeps me on. She believes this Mayfair accent of mine gives the place, as she is wont to say, a bit of class. The woman's a twit, but there you are. But—I tell you this in all honesty, Mrs. Hudson—there was a time when the Latham family could have bought a dozen Burbage Houses, here or in London, and not thought tuppence of it. But such are the vagaries of life that I now find myself—'' He said no more; his hands, raised in a gesture of futility, said it all.

"Life leads us down many a path, does it not, Mr. Latham? And not all of them pleasant, I'm afraid." It was a gratuitous platitude at best but nevertheless seemed apropos to the moment. "But forgive me," I said, "I'm keeping you from your book."

"No, no, that's quite all right," he replied, snapping it shut and resting it on the side table. "It was becoming a bit of a bore, actually."

"You're sure?"

"Yes, quite."

"That being the case," I said, setting mine aside as well, "perhaps you could tell me what you know of Captain Hammond and his wife."

"The Hammonds? Yes, I believe I can. Though there's not that much to tell, really. Seems the old boy was a retired sea captain when he and his wife bought this place some sixty-odd years ago. It was a private home then with the actual dimensions of the house being gradually enlarged over the years. When the Burbages became the new owners some fifteen years ago it was already a tourist home. As to our Captain John Hammond, they say he was quite the character, with many a seafaring tale to tell over a brew or two down at the local pub. A salty old dog who would never tire of telling of the time he lost his good right arm in a skirmish with bloodthirsty corsairs off the Barbary coast. Which, according to him, brought about the end to his life at sea. Which, in itself, makes one wonder."

"As to—?"

"As to whether he ever did hold the rank of captain. I mean, the loss of an arm was never an impediment to Nelson, was it? But that's neither here nor there now. He may have been, as I say, a bit of a character, but from what I can understand he seems to have been well liked by the townsfolk."

"And his wife?"

"Sarah? Mmmm," he mused, "don't know that much about her, actually. A murky figure at best, content to remain in the shadow of her larger-than-life husband. But it's said she simply adored the old boy. The very epitome of the loyal and devoted wife."

I found all that I was hearing to be quite fascinating and mentally congratulated myself for having turned down Vi's offer to accompany her. "And how long," I asked, in pursuing the subject, "did the Hammonds actually live here?"

"It was no more than a year after their moving in," he answered, "when the captain took a tumble down the stairs and broke his neck, poor chap. As for Sarah," he continued "she died but a month later in her bed, never accepting the fact that her husband had passed on."

"Never accepting—? I don't understand."

"They say she went a bit funny—up here," he stated with a tap to his forehead. "Seems she couldn't come to grips with the idea that her husband had actually died and would take to wandering throughout the house calling out to him. Still does, in point of fact," he added with a bemused smile.

"You're not saying you've seen her?"

"Oh, yes, certainly," he answered, as if it were the most natural thing in the world. "The last time being no more than a month or so ago, I should say. In the upstairs hall. But don't look so shocked, Mrs. Hudson." (I suppose I did.) "One becomes accustomed here to that sort of thing over the years. In truth, one really doesn't have any other choice."

I responded by saying I'd be hard-pressed to take the seeing of spiritual beings so lightly, no matter how many times they might manifest themselves. I then questioned him by asking if he had witnessed visitations by her husband as well. He informed me that up until Vi's sighting of him, the captain had not been seen for at least a good five years. And that he himself had been the last person to have witnessed the apparition.

"We all thought," he continued, "the Burbages and I,

that is, that we were at last rid of him. That left us with only Sarah to contend with. But now—'' He paused, remaining silent as he rubbed finger to chin in thought before offering up the word *strange*.

There was that word again. This time I would not let it slip by. "Strange, Mr. Latham?" I questioned. "In what way?"

"This story of Mrs. Warner's," he began again, "and I'm not saying I disbelieve it, mind you, but it doesn't seem to follow a prescribed pattern, so to speak."

"In what sense?"

"Not to put too fine a point on it," he answered, "but the thing of it is, I've done quite a bit of reading up on the subject. And it seems that when a being dies quite unexpectedly, as was the case with the captain, the spirit seems to hover over and around the area of his or her demise. And will continue to do so over the years until at last finding their own particular path to paradise. Why this should be, no one really knows. But take for example Anne Boleyn, who has been seen over the centuries walking the bloody Tower."

"With her head tucked underneath her arm," I added impishly.

"Head or no head," he responded with a smile, "the fact remains, there she was beheaded and there she remains."

"And in the case of Captain Hammond—?"

"In each instance his appearance has always been as a ghostly figure gazing down in mute sorrow at the descending staircase that took his life. But now," he responded, with a bewildered shake of his head, "your Mrs. Warner has seen him in the hallway and has heard his unearthly wanderings in the attic as well. As you see, it is, as I say, all very strange."

"And yet, Mr. Latham," I interjected, "who are we mere mortals to question the coming and going of departed souls simply because they don't happen to conform to our prejudged perception as to how they should react."

"As to how they should react," he repeated softly to himself, as if harboring some secret thought. "What you say," he announced after a moment's pause, "reminds me of a story. Shall I tell it to you?"

"By all means," I answered with a smile. "A ghost story, is it?"

"As to that, I'll leave you to be the judge," he replied, returning the smile. "The tale, reported to be true," he began, "concerns a certain squire who lived on a very grand estate somewhere in the Midlands. And while he was a good husband and family man, he showed little interest in the estate itself. The grounds he left to his grounds-keeper, for he himself wouldn't have known a rose from a ragweed. And though he was the possessor of a fine stable, his interest in horses was negligible. From his walls hung row upon row of some of the finest masterpieces ever seen in a private collection. Though he paid scant attention to them, if at all. But the good squire did have one overriding passion. And that was fishing. Far to the back of his estate ran a stream wherein, according to the squire, resided some of the finest trout in all of England. And not a day would pass that he would not take off alone down a well-worn footpath that snaked its way through the grounds to his beloved stream.

"It was on just such a day that the squire, setting off with tackle box and fishing pole in hand, spotted a man dressed in clothes not seen in the squire's time, coming up the path toward him. 'Hello!' thought the squire. 'Who's this? A poacher?' For the man carried a pole in one hand and a wicker basket in the other. From that basket could be seen the tails of two very large trout hanging out of it. The man continued up the path, head down, with no sign given that he was aware the squire was approaching ever closer.

" 'Who are you, fellow?' cried out the squire. And as he did so, the man stopped, raised his head, and, startled out of his wits on seeing the squire, promptly disappeared! They say the squire became so distraught at having been

confronted by such an apparition he never again returned
to his trout stream nor did he ever fish again.''

"Simply because he had seen a ghost," I said. "How
very sad."

"Ah, but that's the thing of it, Mrs. Hudson," replied
Mr. Latham. "Was it, in fact, a ghost that he saw?"

"If not a ghost, what then?"

"Remember," he reminded me, "the man appeared to
be as startled on seeing the squire as did the squire on
seeing him. Which has led those who have studied the case
to suggest something very different."

"Such as?" I inquired.

"That the man with the trout had, for a brief moment in
time, stumbled into the future, as it were," he replied.
"And would have no more thought of himself as a ghost
as would you or I."

"Then you're saying," I replied, "that to the poacher, it
would appear as if the squire was the ghost."

"Yes, exactly. Mind," he added, "he may not have been
a poacher at all but a previous owner from centuries past."

I shook my head in the wonderment of it all. "The
story," I said, "certainly lends itself to a number of possibilities, doesn't it?"

"It does indeed, Mrs. Hudson," he acknowledged.
"Can't you just imagine each man going home to his wife
that night and each telling of having seen a ghost on the
old footpath that led down to the stream? Whether it be a
ghost or whatever, I suppose only on our final day will the
mysteries of the unknown be revealed to us."

"Needless to say," I replied with a smile, "I'm in no
hurry for the answer."

"Nor am I, dear lady," he replied with some amusement.
"Nor am I."

"One or two more questions, Mr. Latham," I said. "In
regard to the Hammonds. Have they ever appeared together? In spirit form, I mean."

"No, never," he informed me. "It is as if neither one is
aware of the other's presence. The captain," he explained,

"is seen, as I say, for a few seconds or more at the top of the landing; then, and it might be some months later, Mrs. Hammond suddenly appears out of nowhere, seemingly in search of her husband. For she calls out to him in a most pitiful voice of despair. Which has led me to believe they are existing, if that's the right word for it, on two different levels of thought or consciousness."

"How very terrible it all is," I added with a sorrowful sigh, "that they are unable to meet and share their spiritual life together in a world of ever-lasting love."

"Perhaps one day they will, Mrs. Hudson," was his thoughtful reply. "Perhaps one day they will."

"And as to Mrs. Hammond herself," I asked, "what sort of a woman was she? How would you describe her?"

"As for the answer to that," he announced, "you can see for yourself."

"See for myself?" I looked him up and down. "Whatever are you talking about, Mr. Latham?"

"She's right behind you," he replied in all seriousness. "And the captain too, for that matter."

"You're joking!" I said.

"Turn around and see," he said.

I could feel the hair on the nape of my neck standing on end as I grasped the arms of my chair and, very slowly, turned my head to the back of the room. "I see no one!" I exclaimed, now more relieved than alarmed.

"There," he said, pointing to the wall. "The painting just above the table. "A fair likeness, I'd say, of both the captain and his wife."

"A painting! Really, Mr. Latham!" I fumed. "How could you?"

"Do forgive me, Mrs. Hudson," he begged in shame-faced bemusement. "Did I frighten you? Yes, I can see that I did. Again, forgive me, dear lady."

"You're forgiven," I replied, exonerating him with a smile, while mentally castigating myself on having been so gullible.

"Come then," said he, rising from his chair. "Let's take a look, shall we?"

The painting, set within a scrolled gilt frame, was ill-lit and could have easily gone unnoticed. "I believe it was painted by one of our local artists a few months before the captain's death," Mr. Latham informed me on our approach.

Mrs. Hammond, I noticed in stepping forward for a closer inspection, would have been somewhere in her forties. Not pretty, no, but a pleasant-faced woman whom the artist had placed so that she stood slightly to the back and left of her husband in three-quarter profile. The round face, complete with a Mona Lisa wisp-like smile, was framed by ringlets of russet-brown curls. While the eyes of pale green, caught forever in time, gazed lovingly up at him in silent adoration.

My eyes turned toward the likeness of her husband. The artist, I thought, had captured quite nicely the folds of the right arm's empty sleeve. As for the cap pulled low on the forehead, the muttonchop sideburns swept out from the face as if caught by a nor'easter, the jutting chin line, and the eyes squinting off into some unseen horizon—I found to be overly dramatic, and said as much to Mr. Latham.

"Couldn't agree with you more," he replied. "In fact, Sam—Mr. Burbage, that is—has remarked on more than one occasion that the only thing missing is a parrot on his shoulder."

"He does look a character, doesn't he?" I chuckled, stepping back for one last lingering look at the painting. "But," I added, after a pause, "isn't there something—wrong?" I took another step back and continued looking at it this way and that.

"Wrong?" he asked. "In what way wrong?"

"I—I don't know, really. It's just that—oh, it's nothing," I answered, airily dismissing with a wave of my hand whatever it was that was tugging at the back of my mind. "And you say it's been years since you or anyone last saw the captain?"

"Yes," he stated. "At least a good five."

Perhaps it was in the viewing of the painting, I don't know, but for some reason or other, I began to entertain self-doubts. Had I been right in asserting spirits could freely roam where they will, when Mr. Latham was of the opinion that the captain's 'place' was at the top of the stairs? But then, if it wasn't Captain Hammond that Vi had seen, then who? Perhaps, just perhaps, I thought, there might be a mystery here after all.

THREE

A Bump in the Night

⟋⟋⟍IT WAS BUT a few minutes later after my having returned to our room that Vi entered. "Should have come into town with me, Em," she said, depositing a number of parcels down on the bed. "I managed to pick up one or two things—nowt much, mind, souvenirs like. But, oh, the prices! Can't imagine what they'll be asking when it gets more into the tourist season. 'Ere," she added, handing me a small box, "this is for you."

"For me? Oh, Vi, there was no need to get me anything," I replied in surprise at her thoughtful gesture. "What is it? Oh, a sachet!" I exclaimed on bringing forth a small scented bag from its wrapping. "It smells lovely."

"Couldn't see anything for the doctor," she said, "but maybe next time I'm out. But this," she continued on, holding up an undistinguished circular wooden container complete with knobbed lid, "is for Mr. Holmes. It's what they call a humidor. It's for keeping tobacco in so's it won't go all stale-like. See," she beamed on holding it up for examination, "it even has the word *Brighton* written on the side of it in fancy yellow lettering. I think it's right smart, I do. What do you think?"

My face dropped. "It's—it's nice," I answered, managing a small smile for her benefit. "But," I added, knowing only too well what Mr. Holmes would think of it when she presented it to him, "you know, of course, dear, that he keeps his tobacco in the toe of the Persian slipper atop his mantelpiece."

"Well, yes, 'course I do," she retorted, knowing as well as I, it was but one of Mr. Holmes's many idiosyncrasies. "But he won't have to now, will he? I mean," she went on, "who wants to keep tobacco in a slipper what some old Arab has had his foot in, eh?"

"Obviously, Mr. Holmes does," I muttered to myself. Though why he did, I hadn't the foggiest.

"What do you think he'll say when he sees it?" she asked in all eagerness.

"Words will fail him," I replied. And with that, I crossed over to the dresser with the thought of setting the sachet in with my clothes. As I was about to open the drawer I was suddenly engulfed in an unearthly chill. Vi must have noticed my discomfort for she asked whatever was the matter. "I felt as if I had just stepped into an icebox," I replied with a brisk rub to my arms.

"Eh? Howd' you mean?"

"Come over here," I said. "There seems to be a cold spot right—oh, it's gone. Now isn't that strange."

"Could be," ventured Vi, "you're coming down with summat."

"No, I'm fine now," I assured her. "But for a second there it felt as if a cold wind had blown right through me."

"Aye, I shouldn't be surprised," she said. "Draughty old room that it is."

"A draught? Hmmm—I wonder."

"You wonder? 'Bout what?"

"Oh, nothing. Nothing at all, really," I answered. But in truth, a thought had crossed my mind as to why I had suddenly experienced a sudden drop in temperature. But of this, I said nothing, being too frightened or perhaps feeling a little too foolish in voicing my suspicions aloud. I let the matter rest for the present and, setting the sachet aside on the dresser, I inquired of Violet as to how she had gotten along with the Trefanns.

"Oh, well enough, I suppose," she added with a shrug. "They didn't seem all that anxious to strike up a conversation. When we got out of the carriage they went their way and I went mine. Same thing coming back. Nobody said much. Though I remember Mr. Trefann mentioning that he works for the government or some such thing."

"The government? In what capacity?" I asked. Certainly not as a member of Parliament, I thought. It would be more likely they'd be lodged at the Grand, if that were the case.

"I dunno," she replied. "I didn't press him. It's like I say, I didn't feel all that comfortable with them. But what of you, eh?" she questioned, sitting herself down on the side of the bed. "Got a bit of reading done, did you?"

"No, not really," I confessed. "But it did turn out to be an enjoyable if not enlightening afternoon," I added, taking my place on one of the two chairs within the room. I then related my meeting and subsequent conversation I had with Mr. Latham. Including, as I did, the joke played on me by that gentleman in regard to the spirits of the Hammonds who supposedly were standing just behind me. My telling of it evoking peals of laughter from my companion. As indeed it did from myself as well this time around. As to Mr. Latham's knowledge of the Hammonds, Vi listened in rapt attention but, when I spoke of his questioning why the captain, returning as he had after all these years, should go wandering through the hall or, for that matter, take himself up to the attic, Violet was quick to step in. "I should think a ghost could go where he flamin' well wants to!" she stated most forcefully, adding that she ruddy well knew what she had seen.

"There's no need to take it personally," I soothed. "Mr. Latham isn't questioning what you saw, he only finds it all—rather odd."

"Odd—aye, it's that, all right, and no mistake," she heartily agreed. "But 'ere, what of Mrs. Hammond, eh?" she asked. "Whereabouts does she pop up then?"

"Anywhere," I answered, remembering the unearthly chill I had experienced but moments before. "That is to say, anywhere within the confines of this house."

"That's always nice to know, isn't it?" was her sardonic reply, accompanied by a weary yawn.

"You look as if you could use forty winks, m'girl," I said with a smile as she stifled another yawn. "Why not have yourself a bit of a nap? I'll wake you in time for dinner."

"Aye, perhaps I will then," she agreed. "But what about you, eh?"

"I thought I might go down and sit out on the verandah for a while. A bit of fresh air would be just the ticket for me right about now."

"Best take a shawl then," she advised. "And be sure to lock the door behind you when you go. Though," she added, "I suppose a fat lot of good that'll do if the Hammonds decide to float in."

Ordinarily her remark would have garnered a chuckle or two from me, but this time I could but offer up a weak smile. Had I actually experienced a visitation within the room, I wondered on locking the door behind me, or was my brush with the beyond no more than a draught coupled with an overactive imagination? Perhaps, I thought, I would never know.

An intermittent breeze coupled with the waning warmth of the sun greeted me as I stepped out onto the verandah. A verandah, I noted, whose railing and peeling spindles were in dire need of a fresh coat of white paint. As to seating, an odd assortment of chairs, both wooden and wicker, sat with their backs to the window, all empty and waiting save one. In that chair sat Mr. Jones. Seemingly unaware of my presence, he continued to stare aimlessly into space. Should I find a chair for myself far removed from the young man, I thought, or take my place nearer to him? In truth, he interested me. I had never seen him smile. So sullen he was, for one so young. And why had he chosen to come here to Burbage House by himself? I sat down but one chair from him.

"I'm Mrs. Hudson," I said, on his acknowledging my presence by rising slightly from his chair.

"Jones," he replied, forcing a smile. "Peter Jones."

As he made no further attempt at conversation, I took the initiative. "Are you enjoying your stay here in Brighton, Mr. Jones?" I asked. My question received no more than a small shrug. "A foolish question on my part," I said. "I can see that you're not."

"Forgive me, Mrs. Hudson, if I appear uncommunicative, but I'm afraid you'll not find me fit company for man or beast," he replied in a voice that had a decidedly Welsh lilt to it.

"Well then, young sir," said I, "as I don't qualify in either one of those two categories, perhaps you might want to unburden yourself to me as to what it is that troubles you."

"I'd best be keeping myself to myself," he announced after a thoughtful pause. "Though I thank you for your concern."

"Very well, if that's your wish," I stated, adding only that it was my belief that it's difficult to ferret out answers to problems if they're kept bottled up inside.

I received no reply.

We continued to sit in silence. He, staring morosely out into the clouds and thinking who knows what, and I, basking in the breeze and enjoying the scent of sea air. It was a reverie that was at last broken by the young man's unexpected and most startling admission.

"I'm on my honeymoon," he said.

"You're what?" I gasped, searching his face for perhaps a flicker of a smile but finding none.

"Honeymoon," he repeated. "Though a belated one at that."

"Mr. Jones," was my bewildered response, "whatever are you talking about?"

"I suppose it does sound queer," he answered. "But the thing of it is, see, we were married a year ago this month, my Cathie and me." At this point, he pursed his lips in thought as if unsure whether or not to continue.

"Do go on, Mr. Jones," I urged him. "I'm most interested."

"Are you? Yes," he said, with eyes searching deep into mine, "I can see that you are. It's just that," he began again, "at the time, we never had so much as two farthings to rub together. But we made a promise, we did, that next year we'd have ourselves a proper honeymoon. And what with Cathie working in the millinery shop and me as a printer's assistant and taking on whatever odd jobs I could at night, we finally scrimped enough together for the trip."

"But I don't understand," I said. "If that's the case, where is—?"

"Cathie? We had what you might call a bit of a tiff the night before we were to leave. With terrible words being said on both sides, I'm sorry to say. The outcome of it being her refusal to accompany me to Brighton."

"And so you came down here leaving her on her own in London, is that it?"

"Well," he explained, "I thought she'd follow me, didn't I."

So, it was the absence of his wife due to a lovers' quarrel that had produced his state of melancholia. Still, I was curious about one thing. "Tell me, Mr. Jones," I asked, "what was it that made you at last decide to confide in me?"

"It's like you were saying, Mrs. Hudson," he answered. "It's no good keeping it all inside. Besides, I couldn't help in thinking how much you remind me of my great-aunt Gwen. She was like a second mother to me and my four brothers when our own passed away. A good woman she was, who always took the time to listen to our problems no matter how foolish they might have been."

"I'm flattered by the comparison," I replied. As indeed I was. "Originally from Wales then, are you?" I asked.

He stated that he was. "From a little mining town, the name of which you've never heard of or, for that matter, could even pronounce if it came to that," he added with a lopsided grin. "I had no stomach for working the mines, see. Like digging your own grave, it is. So I set off for London where I eventually met Cathie."

"I see. And speaking of your wife," I asked, "you've not heard from her since arriving at Burbage's—no letter?"

"Not a line," was his dejected response.

"But you've written her yourself, haven't you?"

"Why, no," he stated. "I've sent no letter." He seemed surprised by the question.

"So," I said, "here you sit in Brighton and there she sits in London. Each one waiting for the other to make the first move. Is that the game? Well, if it is, m'lad, it's a game with no winners." He was about to respond but I cut him short. "Now you listen to me, Mr. Peter Jones," I said, addressing him in a no-nonsense tone of voice, "you take pen in hand the minute you get back to your room and see that the letter gets off to London first thing in the morning."

He vowed he would do just that.

The conversation then turned to the Hammonds. A topic, he informed me, that he had only recently been made aware of by Mrs. Burbage. "Ah, yes," I answered, "she did say as how she would mention it to you and the others. And do you," I went on, "believe that their ghostly spirits still reside within the halls of Burbage House?"

"I do," he stated straight-out.

"Do you indeed?" It was an answer I had not expected. For a belief in the beyond is not usually associated with those of Mr. Jones's generation. Death and whatever it is that may or may not lay ahead they leave to the aged to ponder over. For to be young is to be immortal. "And is there any particular reason for your belief?" I asked, wondering if he himself had seen or been visited by either the captain or his wife.

"There is, Mrs. Hudson," he answered. "It's my mother, see. On the night before I left for London I was awakened by a vision of her at the foot of my bed. I'd like to think," he added quietly, "that she had come to wish me well."

"As no doubt she did," I replied, leaning over to rest my hand on his arm in a gesture of comfort.

We then lapsed into generalities with respect to the weather and various other sundry subjects until twilight's lengthening shadows reminded me of my own vow to wake Vi in time for dinner. I stood up, said my goodbyes, and once more reminded him to write to his wife.

"But what will I say?" He posed the question almost in a whine.

"What's this?" I replied, addressing him in mock admonishment. "A newlywed like yourself asking an old woman like me what it is he should say to his young wife? Really, Mr. Jones!"

Later that night as Vi and I set about retiring for bed, I suddenly noticed something that set me aback, if not in surprise, then certainly in puzzlement. I turned to my companion who, seated by the bed, was in the midst of applying great gobs of cream to her face. "Vi," I asked, "that sachet you gave me, did you see what I did with it?"

"Put it on the dresser, didn't you, luv?" she asked, now in the process of massaging her creamed cheeks.

"That's what I thought," I answered as I continued to scan the top of it. "But it seems to have disappeared."

"Disappeared?" She came over to inspect for herself. "Well, *I* don't know what you've done with it," she said. "Did you put it in your purse?"

"My purse!" I exclaimed. "Why on earth would I put it in my purse?"

"'Ere, how should I know?" she snapped. "Just trying to be helpful, I was."

"I was standing by the dresser just before I left for my outing on the verandah," I announced, trying to relive the scene, "with the thought in mind of placing it in the drawer. But with that cold spot I felt at the time I simply placed it on top of the dresser. I'm sure I did."

"Why not look in the drawer just in case then?" she asked.

"There's as much chance of finding it in there as in my purse," I retorted.

"Well, you won't know 'til you look, will you?"

I slid the drawer out. "I don't believe it!" I cried out in bewilderment. For there atop my unmentionables sat the sachet. "But . . . but . . ." I spluttered, "I don't remember—."

"Humph," humphed Vi, "forget where you put your head, you would. Either that or," she added with a wink, "talking to that nice Mr. Jones you were telling me about has left you all a-twitter."

"Oh, for heaven's sake, Violet," I responded with annoyance, "don't talk so foolish." But I *had* left it on top of the dresser. I felt more than certain I had. But then how—? A mental picture of Sarah Hammond immediately flashed before me. No, I told myself, I'd not travel down the path of paranoia by my believing every odd occurrence was caused by that departed soul. Perhaps Vi had been right. Perhaps I *had* set it inside the drawer and the act of doing so had slipped my mind, though in truth I didn't believe I had. However, I believed it best that I keep my thoughts to myself. I knew only too well the reaction I'd receive from Vi if I announced my belief that Sarah Hammond had a ghostly hand in it. But little did I realize, as I settled myself down in bed, that before morning's light the now not-so-mysterious movement of sachet from dresser top to drawer would fade into insignificance by a happening far more physical in nature.

Sometime during the early hours of the morning (I put the time at around two or two-thirty) we were again awakened by sounds coming from the attic. "He's at it again," grumbled Vi, rising up from beneath the counterpane. I sat myself up alongside her. "Yes, so it would seem," I answered, with the thought occurring to me, ironic as it was, that we were now accepting spiritual shufflings from above more in annoyance than from an overriding sense of fear. Indicating to me, at least, that human beings can adapt themselves to almost anything if it's carried out on a continual basis.

"He's making more than a bit of a ruckus tonight, I'll say that for him," added a now more irritable Violet.

Before I could respond one way or the other, we caught the sound of a very distinctive and uncommonly loud thump from above. I threw the covers aside and bounded out of bed.

" 'Ere, what's all this, then?" cried Vi. "Where are you off to, eh?"

"That was no ghost, m'girl," I announced, throwing on my housecoat. "That was the sound of someone very human falling to the floor."

"Well," she said, "that may be as is, but you're not thinking of going up there, are you?"

"This has gone on long enough!" I stated, now more angry then annoyed. "You're more than welcome to come along or not," I continued, in the faint hope that she would (I'm not all that brave). "It's up to you."

"Well, if it comes to that," she answered, throwing back the counterpane and swinging her feet out onto the floor, "I suppose it's best if we stick together. But," she added, "don't you think it might be best-like if we woke up one of the men? That Mr. Jones is a big strapping bloke."

"We don't have time," I stated most impatiently from my stance by the now half open door. "And do get a move on, Violet."

"All right, all right, then," she mumbled. "Can't wait 'til a body gets into her slippers, can you?"

Ready at last, we stepped out into the hallway and immediately bumped into the rotund Mr. Burbage who, in his nightgown of white, looked for all the world like a single-masted schooner in full sail. "You heard it, too?" he asked, as the oil lamp he had brought along continued to cast us in a series of eerie shadows.

"Aye," said Vi. "Couldn't help but not hear it, could we? Em and I are just on our way up to see what it's all about."

"Oh, I wouldn't do that if I were you," he advised. "Best you two go back to your room. Ol' Sam Burbage will handle it from here on in, he will. Never know what you'll see up there."

"Quite right, Mr. Burbage," I replied. "We never will know, will we, if we don't see for ourselves. Now then, if you'd be kind enough to lead the way, we'd be much obliged."

Reluctantly, our host led us down the hallway to where it sharp-angled to the left. At which point, we turned and carried on but a few feet more to where a partially open attic door, as if daring us to enter, lay in wait. Mr. Burbage paused, as if having second thoughts as to whether or not he should continue on. "Shall I lead?" I asked. "Or will you?"

With a scowl and a mumbling of words under his breath, he eased back the door and proceeded, as quietly as he could, to make his way up the creaking staircase. We, in turn, followed suit. "There's nothing up here but a lot of old junk from what I can make out," he announced in a whisper, holding, as he did, the lamp aloft as we entered. "Dorie's always after me, she is, to clean it up. But I ask you, what's the use, eh? Don't see why—" He stopped in mid-sentence and emitted a sharp gasp. As did we. For we each had heard a movement of sorts to the back of the attic.

"There's someone up here," quavered Vi, " 'sides us."

"Who's there?" I cried out into the darkness.

"Is that you, Mrs. Hudson?" questioned a voice from somewhere deep within the room.

" 'Ere, who's that then?" sang out Vi, experiencing, as (no doubt) Mr. Burbage and I did, a small measure of relief on the hearing of a human voice rather than that of a ghostly one. With Mr. Burbage and his lamp leading the way, we advanced forward to find our mysterious intruder gazing up at us with frightened eyes from his crouched position on the floor. "Why, it's our Mr. Jones!" exclaimed Violet.

"The lamp this way, if you will, Mr. Burbage," I said, ignoring Mr. Jones for the moment on seeing the shadowy figure of yet another man that lay uncommonly still beside him. Mr. Burbage stepped forward. The light afforded us by his lamp opened up a scene that left we who viewed it with a sense of utter astonishment, if not horror. There, staring up at me with open, unseeing eyes, lay the body of Mr. Latham. Dear, sweet Mr. Latham. Dead. I couldn't believe it. I reached out for Vi's arm to steady myself.

"Good God, Jones!" Mr. Burbage at last managed to splutter out. "What have you done?"

"I've done nothing—nothing!" the man exclaimed, springing to his feet.

Vi was quick to respond. "Murdered Mr. Latham, that's what you've done. Call that nowt, do you?"

"I've murdered no one," he declared in an obvious state of agitation. "You've got to believe me—all of you."

"Oh, yes?" questioned Mr. Burbage, looking him up and down. "And why should we have to do that then, eh?"

"Because it's the truth!" the other man shot back.

"Perhaps," I said, stepping in, "we should give Mr. Jones the opportunity of explaining his presence here."

"Thank you for that at least, Mrs. Hudson," he answered before exhaling a sigh of relief.

"Well, get on with it then, man!" fumed Mr. Burbage.

"I suppose," he began, "it all started somewhere around two o'clock this morning. Being unable to sleep, I got up and took a chair by the window. I was about to light a cigarette when I heard this great thump from above. 'Now, that's queer,' I thought. So, with nothing better to do, I decided to come up here to investigate."

"Didn't think it could have been Captain Hammond then, eh?" questioned Vi.

"No, not really," he answered. "Oh, I'd heard the odd noises before at night and knew about the Hammonds from what Mrs. Burbage had told me, but this, now—this seemed more human, see. So I came up and, in stumbling about, as I did, from what light there is available from that little window in back, I came upon poor Mr. Latham lying there where you see him now. I bent down over him, thinking him to be unconscious and that I might be able to help in some way. That's when I saw he was dead. Then, when I heard footsteps leading upstairs and saw a light being shined about, I stayed crouched where I was, see. Not knowing who it was 'til I heard Mrs. Hudson call out."

"Expect us to believe that, do you?" sneered the other man.

"But Mr. Burbage," I countered, "is that not exactly the reason why we ourselves are here? Did we not each hear a noise and come up to investigate?"

"Well," he grumbled, "I don't know what to make of it all then."

"Nor do I," I replied. "But perhaps I might be able to offer up a few answers," I added, managing as I did so to place myself into a kneeling position beside the body.

"Why, whatever are you looking for?" queried Mr. Jones.

"The reason for his death," I replied before gently closing the lids over those lifeless eyes.

"Mrs. Hudson here is what you might call a detective," announced Mr. Burbage, addressing Mr. Jones in a voice that indicated self-satisfaction in being privy to the information. Mr. Jones expressed surprise. "Why, she and Mr. Sherlock Holmes have solved many a murder together," added the older man. "Isn't that right, Mrs. Hudson?"

"No," I stated sharply. "It is not." Thereby quickly deflating him into an embarrassed silence. "We heard no shot so we can rule out the possibility of gunplay," I mused aloud as I continued in my examination of the body. "And," I added, on checking out the chest area, "I find no knife wound present. Ah, here," I said, seeing a small pool of blood to the back of the head, "here's the answer. Could you bring the lamp a little closer, Mr. Burbage?" I asked, for I had also noticed that one of the four cast-iron legs of an old sewing machine table that sat to the back of Mr. Latham's head had a dark splotch of red on it. As he did so, I dabbed a finger to it and found it sticky. "A hand up, if you please, Mr. Jones," I requested of the man who then very nicely obliged. "It would appear," said I to one and all on rising, "that Mr. Latham's death was caused by taking a fall and striking his head against the cast-iron leg of the sewing machine."

"But what or who caused him to fall, eh?" asked Vi, with an eye toward Mr. Jones. "That's what I'd like to know."

"Mr. Burbage!" sang out Mrs. Burbage, making her appearance with candle in hand upon the threshold of the attic door. "Whatever is going on up here?" she demanded to know of the man. "It seems you've managed to wake up the entire household!" And, so saying, in marched the lady of the house accompanied in turn by the Trefanns bringing up the rear. "What nonsense have you been up to now?" she asked in a belligerent tone of voice. Then, without waiting for a reply, she set about offering up her apologies to those of us assembled, on behalf of her husband. "For the life of me," she said, "I don't know why Mr. Burbage—"

"It's Mr. Latham, Dorie," interjected her husband, holding his lamp aloft over the sprawled body on the floor. "He's dead."

His wife let out a gasp, put her hand over her mouth, and remained momentarily speechless. Mr. Trefann took a step forward, the better to view the remains, then stepped back quickly to take hold of his wife who looked as if she was about to swoon. Dora Burbage shook her head in disbelief. "I don't understand," she spoke at last, turning to her husband. "Was it a heart attack?"

"Mrs. Hudson here," he answered, "says he fell and

cracked his head on that old sewing machine table of yours.''

"My sewing machine! And how many times," she asked, spewing out the words, "have I asked you to get rid of it? But oh, no, pay no never-mind to me, you don't."

He offered up no reply.

"But what would Mr. Latham be doing up here in the first place?" asked Mr. Trefann of no one in particular.

"You and Mrs. Trefann heard no noises earlier this night?" I questioned.

"No," he said, turning to his wife for confirmation and receiving it by a negative shake of her head. "We're both sound sleepers. But," he added, "we did awake when we heard you people up here. Wondering what was up, we poked our heads out the door and caught sight of Mrs. Burbage coming down the hall."

"She mentioned she was on her way up to the attic to see what it was that was keeping her husband," spoke Mrs. Trefann. "Being curious, we followed her up."

"I say," added Mr. Trefann, with an eye toward the body, "shouldn't he—you know, be covered up or something?"

"Quite right," I agreed. "Perhaps Mr. Burbage here might be able to find some sort of blanket to—oh, my heavens!" I cried out with a start.

"What is it? What's the matter, Em?" exclaimed Vi.

"Something just brushed by my ankle," I managed to gasp out. Being too frightened to move, I stood stock-still, wondering whether or not to look down.

"Why, it's old Mrs. Barnaby," announced Mrs. Burbage.

"Mrs. who?" was my bewildered response as I mentally pictured some elderly woman at my feet writhing madly about on the floor.

"Our cat," spoke Mr. Burbage, as his wife bent down to pick up a large, furry, orange-brown feline.

"Why, I've never known her to come up here before," said Mrs. Burbage, cuddling the calico cat in her arms.

"Bad ol' Mrs. Barnaby," she cooed with a tap of her finger to its wet nose. "Frightened poor Mrs. Hudson, you did."

"Perhaps for the moment," I mumbled, feeling a trifle foolish.

"Will this be all right, Mrs. Hudson?" asked Mr. Burbage, holding up a grey woolen blanket for inspection.

"I don't see why not," I answered, grateful for the change in subject.

"Doubt if Mr. Latham will care one way or t'other, in any case, poor old soul," added Violet.

"Mr. Burbage," I asked, after his placing of the blanket over the body, "I believe you've a telephone downstairs, have you not?"

"Indeed I do, Mrs. Hudson," he replied with a touch of pride to his voice.

I replied that it might best be put to use by ringing the local constabulary to inform them of what had taken place. Adding that as there was no further need for any of us to remain up here any longer, we might take ourselves downstairs to await the police.

"Surely there's no need to miss whatever sleep there is remaining to us by awaiting the police," spoke Mr. Trefann.

"As we have a dead man lying on the floor no more than two feet away from where we now stand," I replied, "I think it's safe to assume the police will have a question or two for all concerned. Routine though it may be."

Evidently my reply had the desired effect for, in a body, they turned and began trooping downstairs. As they did, I drew Mrs. Burbage aside to question that lady as to whether she noticed if any of the contents of the room had been moved about in any way.

"Good Lord, Mrs. Hudson," she replied, "how in the world would I know? It's been years since I was last up here."

"Yes, of course." I nodded in understanding. "I should have—oops, sorry," I said, offering up an apology to whoever it was I had just bumped an arm against. Mrs. Trefann? Vi? I didn't turn round to see.

Mrs. Burbage looked at me with the oddest little smile on her face. "Mrs. Hudson," she said, "you've just apologized to a mannequin."

"What!" At that, I turned round to see the fully clothed figure of an alabaster body, with arms akimbo, staring back at me with eyes as sightless as those of Mr. Latham's. "It seems we have more than one body up here, doesn't it?" I joked, in an effort to cover up my embarrassment. Mrs. Burbage did not seem all that amused. "Wherever did you get it?" I asked, for something to say, if nothing else.

"Sam—Mr. Burbage—bought it for me," I was informed, "at some such auction or whatever. Believing I could make use of it in the making of dresses. Never knowing, of course," she went on, "that it was a dressmaker's dummy I needed, not a mannequin. I soon put him right on that." (I've no doubt she did.) "Men," she added in a show of exasperation. "What do they know?"

As we were the last to leave, I went first, with the mistress of Burbage House, with lighted candle held on high, following close behind.

Well now, Emma Hudson, thought I, as we descended the narrow staircase, you couldn't have looked more foolish tonight if you had tried. First the encounter with the cat and then the offering up of apologies to a store-window mannequin. I could only hope I'd fare better with the police.

FOUR

Sarah

ONCE DOWNSTAIRS, ON Mrs. Burbage's suggestion we trundled into the dining room. Rather than sitting together as a group, we each, as if following some unwritten rule of protocol, headed directly to those tables assigned to us for mealtime dining. So there we sat, a roomful of sleepy-eyed individuals looking perfectly ridiculous in our nighttime attire as we awaited the police.

Thankfully, it wasn't long before an inspector, a sergeant, two constables, and another man, whom I was later to learn was the coroner, arrived on the scene. The inspector, after a private word or two with our host from outside the room and a quick look round at we who awaited him within, headed upstairs with Mr. Burbage leading the way. They, in turn, being followed by the inspector's four-man entourage.

"All I can say," muttered Vi, edging her chair closer to mine, "is what with ghosts walking the halls and a dead man in the attic, this has turned out to be some holiday, this has."

"It was your idea to stay," I replied.

"Yours, too," she reminded me.

After what seemed an interminable length of time, though I doubt if it was actually more than fifteen minutes, we heard the sound of heavy-booted feet coming down the stairs. "Look, there goes Mr. Latham," spoke Vi on seeing the blanketed body of the man being carried past our line of vision and out the front door by the two constables. The coroner was next to follow them out. That left the inspector and his sergeant, who now entered the dining room, accompanied by Mr. Burbage announcing to one and all that Inspector Radcliffe would appreciate a moment of our time. Radcliffe? The name sounded familiar but I let it pass.

The inspector, a nondescript man of average height and weight (though a slight paunch was visible beneath the three-buttoned coat), removed his hat, held it to his side, and addressed the assembly. "I thank you for your patience, ladies and gentlemen," he said. "And I promise I shan't keep you any longer than need be must. I'm sure," he went on, "that you'd much rather be in your beds." There was a murmur of agreement from among the guests. "I take it we're all here then?" he added, turning to Mrs. Burbage.

"Everyone except the Christies," she informed him.

That's right, I thought, I'd completely forgotten about them.

"The Christies?" queried the inspector. "And where would they be then?"

"Still asleep in their room, like as not," answered Mr. Burbage. "I could go up and wake them and have them come down if you like," he volunteered.

"No need, really," replied the inspector casually enough. "If they've slept through it all, there's not much, if anything, they could tell us in any event. Now then," he continued, "before we get on with it, I understand we have the lady assistant to the famous Sherlock Holmes seated somewhere among us."

I received the most incredulous looks from the Trefanns as I, without thinking, foolishly raised my hand in schoolgirl fashion before immediately bringing it down again.

"Ah," he said, honing in on me, "Mrs. Hudson, isn't it?"

"It is, Inspector." "But," I added, "as to my being Mr. Holmes's assistant, I'm afraid you're mistaken. That gentleman is a lodger in my home."

"But you do follow the same line of—work, shall we say?"

"On occasion," I replied. "But how—?"

"Mr. Burbage," he answered. He need say no more.

"Might have known it'd be Burbage," muttered Vi, in an aside.

"In any event, Mrs. Hudson, I shall be most interested in anything you may have to say in regard to the matter at hand," added the inspector pleasantly enough with a smile.

I returned the smile with one of my own. And why not? I have not always been so fortunate in finding favor with officialdom. "Thank you, Inspector," I said.

"Not at all. Now then," he continued, addressing Mr. Burbage, "I believe, sir, you were telling me earlier about being awakened by hearing some sort of loud bang from the attic. What time would that have been? Take all this down, would you, Styles?" he asked of his sergeant. "Yes, go on, Mr. Burbage."

"I'd say it was 'bout two o'clock or thereabouts," answered the man. "But as to it being a loud bang, it was more like a heavy thump, you might say. Dorie—Mrs. Burbage, that is—heard it too. Thinking I'd best take myself up to the attic for a look-see, I hops out of bed faster than you can say 'Bob's your uncle,' grabs my lamp, and heads out into the hall. That's where I met the ladies, Mrs. Hudson and Mrs. Warner."

Our table now became the focus of the inspector's attention. "And you ladies," he asked, "were out in the hall because—?"

"We had been awakened earlier by hearing what seemed to be scuffling noises coming from above," I said. "Then, on hearing a loud thump, well, that was too much. We decided to do a little investigating on our own.''

"Was that wise?" he asked.

"In hindsight, probably not," I replied.

"Leastways," added Vi, "it weren't no ghost what made the noise. Em and I were sure of that."

"Ghost?" sputtered the man. "Did you say *ghost?*"

"It would seem, Inspector," I answered, "that the spirits of the original owners still walk the halls of Burbage House."

"As Mrs. Warner herself and many a guest over the years will testify to," stated Mrs. Burbage, as she continued to cradle the cat in her arms.

"You might add my name to that list as well," spoke Mr. Trefann.

Mrs. Burbage, as did we all, turned our attention to that gentleman in genuine surprise. "What!" she exclaimed. "You've seen them too?"

"I speak only of the captain," he answered. "Captain Hammond, in the hall. As I recall," he added, "it was during the night of the same day you had spoken to us about their presence."

"That's right," confirmed his wife. "My husband was quite shaken up about it, as well he might be!" Seemingly somewhat embarrassed by her sudden outburst, she slunk down in her chair and said no more.

"But Mr. Trefann," questioned Dora Burbage, "why did you never mention this?"

"There never seemed to be an opportune time," he answered. "Until now."

"Yes, all very interesting I'm sure, ladies and gentlemen," spoke the inspector. "But as for myself, not being a believer in the great beyond, perhaps we might continue on where we left off. Now then, Mrs. Hudson, when you, Mr. Burbage, and Mrs. Warner entered the attic, who was it exactly that found the deceased?"

"What we found exactly," Vi informed him before I had a chance to reply, "was Mr. Jones bending over the body of Mr. Latham. That's him there," she said, pointing to the young man seated at his table who, up to that point, had remained uncommonly quiet throughout the proceedings. With Vi intimating some sort of involvement on his part, he reacted in dramatic fashion by springing up from his table and, in the process, knocking over his chair.

"I had nothing to do with his death!" he cried out. "I'd only come up a minute or two before they and the others had arrived, see. I thought I might be able to help the poor man. I had no way of knowing he was already dead."

"Steady on there, young fellow, m'lad," soothed the inspector. "No need to be upsetting yourself. You're not being charged with any crime. Nor," he added, "is anyone else."

" 'Ere," whispered Vi, "what's the inspector mean—'nor is anyone else'?"

"I think you'll find the death is to be ruled accidental," I whispered back.

"What we have here," spoke the inspector, addressing one and all, "is a clear case of accidental death." I gave Vi a self-satisfied nudge to her side. "What seems to have happened," he went on, "is that Mr. Latham, being awakened by the same scuffling noises you had heard earlier, Mrs. Hudson, came up to the attic to investigate the cause. We found no lamp, lit or unlit, so we can only assume in his haste to arrive on the scene he took none with him. Stumbling about in the darkness, he no doubt tumbled over something that sent him falling backwards where he unfortunately hit the back of his head on the iron leg of the sewing machine's table. Cracking the base of his skull in the process. And from what Mr. Burbage told me earlier, Mrs. Hudson," he added, "I believe you found blood on the leg as well." I nodded that I had. "According to the coroner," he continued, "the fall might even have been induced by a heart attack. The heavy thump that was heard was the sound of his body hitting the floor."

"That's all very well, I'm sure," spoke Vi. "But what of the noise he heard that sent him up there in the first place, eh?"

"To my way of thinking," interjected young Mr. Jones, "it was the ghost of Captain Hammond prowling about, see. And Mr. Latham, seeing it and all, fell back in fright, striking his head."

"Yes, well, no offense, Mr. Jones," replied the inspector, "but it's not what I think. Noises in the attic, is it? Shouldn't doubt it for a moment in an old house such as this. Rats scurrying about, most likely. Or a bird who manages to get in and in its frightened flight to get out knocks something over. Who knows?"

"Well, there's something I'd like to know, Inspector," stated a defensive Mrs. Burbage. "In the first place, you'll find no rats in our attic—or anywhere else for that matter. As to it being a bird, how would it get in? We've but one window up there and it was nailed shut years ago."

"If not a bird or rat," replied the inspector all too smugly, with an eye toward a certain Mrs. Barnaby, "perhaps then a cat?"

And on that note, Inspector Radcliffe, satisfied that the death of Mr. Latham was accidental in nature (and for all I knew at the time it might very well have been so), brought our little meeting to a close.

No sooner had he and his trusty sergeant taken their leave than Mrs. Burbage lashed out at her husband. "How could you have just stood there and said nothing?" she railed. "Why," she added, "he as good as said Mrs. Barnaby was the cause of poor Mr. Latham's death."

Mr. Burbage looked uncommonly uncomfortable by his wife's sudden outburst. "He just meant it could have happened that way," he answered in an attempt to reason with his wife. "I don't think—"

"No," she cut in, "you *don't* think, do you? That's your trouble, that is. You know as well as I," she carried on, "it's ghosts we have in the attic, not cats—or rats, if it comes to that."

"If you ask me," interjected Vi, "I'll wager there's some what think they'd rather have the odd rat or two running around than some bloomin' ghost."

"I speak of things that are, not as we would like them to be, Mrs. Warner," replied Mrs. Burbage in tight-lipped fashion.

By now, we had all risen as a body and were in the process of making our way out of the room. "Just goes to show how wrong a person can be," spoke Vi as we led the way toward the lobby. "I thought Mr. Jones had summat to do with it, but according to the inspector, everything's on the up and up."

"If he's satisfied," I replied, "I daresay that's all that matters."

"You're coming up, are you?" she asked, seeing I had paused in my steps for a look to the back of me.

"In a minute," I answered. "You go on ahead if you want. I'd like to see if I can have a word or two with the Trefanns before they return to their room."

"Right you are, luv. See you upstairs then."

The Burbages were already ascending the stairs with the calico cat following close behind. I watched in some amusement as, unbeknownst to Mrs. Burbage, the slippered foot of her husband shot out and gave the furry little creature a decidedly nasty kick. Understandable, I supposed, at least from that gentleman's point of view. As I maintained my stance within the doorway Mr. Jones, with a nod of his head in passing, bade me good night before retreating, as had Vi, down the hall toward the staircase. As the Trefanns stepped from dining room to lobby I turned to face them. I couldn't have, if asked, given any specific reason for wanting to speak to them, only that something just didn't sit right with me. Not with them necessarily, but as to the events as a whole that both Vi and I had experienced since our arrival at Burbage House. I was of the opinion that if something was amiss, then it might be wise to get, as they say, a better handle on those who resided within. "It's been quite a night, has it not?" I said, putting the question to them before either had a chance to offer up their good nights.

"What? Oh, yes, I daresay it has," answered Mr. Trefann, a short, spare, balding man somewhere in his mid-forties. "Terrible tragedy."

Seeing they were about to continue on, I stepped slightly to the front of them as unobtrusively as I could in the hope of engaging them further in conversation. "Down from London then, are you?" I asked, this time directing my attention and my question to his wife. Mrs. Trefann, of an age approximate to that of her husband, was a thin, pinch-faced woman with mousy brown hair who stood hovering timidly by his side. An earlier description of her by Vi was that of a woman who looked as if she wouldn't say boo to a flea. She had obviously engaged in the nighttime ritual of freeing her hair prior to retiring. Normally worn in a roll, it now hung down most unflatteringly past her shoulders where it ended just below the small of her back. I relate this only as a description, not as a criticism. (Lord knows I fare no better in appearance myself at that early hour of the morning.)

"Yes, from London, that's right," she said. Nothing more. Nothing less.

I was getting nowhere.

I tried again. "Mrs. Warner tells me you have a position of some importance within the government," I said, putting the question to her husband in the hope of drawing him out.

"I should like to think I do," he answered in all earnestness. "Though perhaps not so exciting a one as yours, I'll wager," he added, no doubt in reference to the inspector's earlier announcement of my connection with a certain well-known detective. "Tell me," he asked, "what's this bloke Holmes really like, eh? How would you describe him?"

How many times have I been asked that question? I wondered. "Dedicated," was my one-word response. Realizing it was now I who was answering his questions I sought to put things back on track by asking what exactly was his function in Her Majesty's government. He had said it was an important one. An aide to the Prime Minister? An assistant to the Home Secretary? I doubted it.

"The lifeblood of the Empire, that's what I am, Mrs. Hudson," he proudly announced. "Me and those just like me."

"Some sort of courier then, are you?" I asked, hazarding a guess. "In the diplomatic corps, perhaps?"

"Why, bless you, Mrs. Hudson," he chortled. "Nothing so grand as that, I'm afraid. But my route does encompass Ten Downing Street. And many an important letter I've dropped off at that residence from countries half of which I've never heard of—but important, mind. Some sealed with wax, they are."

I was left completely stunned. "You're a postman," I blurted out.

"That's right." He beamed. "And proud of it."

"As well you should be," I agreed. Though I had never heard of the position being described in such a grandiose manner.

"Shouldn't we best be getting off to bed now, Harold?" asked his wife in her small whispery voice.

"Why, yes," he said. "I suppose we should, Mrs. T."

"I'll follow you up then, if you don't mind," I added.

"Safety in numbers, is that it?" he asked. "Don't blame you at all, Mrs. Hudson, I don't. Not after what I went through the other night. Not seen him yourself, have you?"

"The captain? No, not I," I replied. "It would seem that among the guests only you and Mrs. Warner have had that honor."

"Honor, you say? I don't know about that. But see him I did, and no mistake," he stated most emphatically. I was about to ask him if he might relate his experience, but there was no need for he plunged right into it. "I'd been sitting up in our room reading for the better part of the night," he began, "when, what with my eyes getting blurry and all, I decided it was time to turn in. Hattie here," he added, indicating his wife, "had gone to bed sometime earlier and was fast asleep. Ain't that right, Hattie?"

"Fast asleep," she stated.

"When I went to lock the door," he continued, "I found the key wouldn't fit in proper-like. So I opened the door for a look-see at the lock from the other side. No sooner had I stepped out than I saw him. At the end of the hall where it turns down toward the attic. Staring back at me he was, with this horrible little grin on his face. And looking for all the world just like that painting of himself downstairs. Have you seen it—the painting?" I answered that I had, with the thought of it bringing back memories of the dear, departed Mr. Latham. But of this, I said nothing. "I wasted no time, I can tell you," he went on, "in getting back inside and propping a chair up under the doorknob. Woke the missus up right away, I did. And oh, wasn't I as white as a sheet. Hattie will tell you right enough."

"White as a sheet he was," I was doubly and dutifully informed by his wife.

"I can well understand how you would be," I replied, adding that such a ghostly encounter as he had described would not be one I would have liked to have taken part in.

"I can tell you this," he stated quite emphatically, "it's not something I'd wish on either friend or foe, Mrs. Hudson."

With nothing more to be said on the subject, we proceeded up the stairs. After a moment's pause at the top of the landing to catch my breath, I carried on, stopping only to exchange a final good night with the Trefanns outside their door. With their closing of it I now stood alone in that dimly lit corridor. And though I know not the why of it, for the first time in the many times I'd walked that same hallway since arriving at Burbage's, I felt truly frightened.

Was it some sort of eerie premonition I was experiencing, I wondered, or was it merely an overreaction on my part to Mr. Trefann's haunting tale of a grinning ghost? Whatever the reason, I told myself, I'd best get a move on. Our room was but a few steps down and, once inside, all would be well. I quickened my pace. But after having taken no more than a few steps, I stopped dead in my tracks with a heart palpitating to such an extent that I put my hand to it as if the act of doing so would reduce its quickening beat. For I had seen within the flickering shadows someone or something quietly approaching.

I stood rooted to the spot, awash in a state of unbridled fear, before giving in, just as quickly, to a sigh of heartfelt relief. For as the apparition drew nearer I could now make out the figure to be that of a woman. Vi! Of course; it had to be. The dear thing, no doubt worried by my prolonged absence, had left her bed to see why I had not as yet returned to our room. As she made no effort to address me, I could only assume that, although gladdened by the sight of me, she was, just as equally, harboring an annoyance with my tardiness. As she passed by the solitary gas lamp on the wall, not only was I once again enveloped in an unearthly chill, but I could now see that the woman who I had first perceived to be Violet Warner was none other than Sarah Hammond! Why I didn't immediately drop to the floor in a dead faint, I shall never know.

Looking back on it, the only answer I can give for not doing so is that the woman looked so very real. Being, as I am, well versed in the tales of Edgar Allan Poe, perhaps I had expected to encounter a skull-like head with socketless eyes encased in a face of rotted flesh. But, thankfully enough, this spiritual entity was, as I say, a fully three-dimensional being. With but one exception. In the area just below the knees, the full, floor-length dress of grey faded away into nothingness, like that of some unfinished painting. We were now no more than half an arm's length away from each other as she passed, or perhaps I should say, glided by. She seemed preoccupied in thought and unaware of my presence.

Her face, now more visible to me as she came within my line of vision, was clearly one of anguish. "John, John, John," she repeated, over and over again in her continuance down the hall. As the sound of her voice began to fade into the distance, I somehow managed to screw up enough courage to turn around for one last look. What I saw set me

completely a-tingle. Her body, now with no more substance
to it than candle smoke, began to evaporate into the air
until at last she was no more.

After that, I vaguely recall scurrying down the hall to
the sanctity of our room. I have no memory of even un-
dressing for bed. Nor of Vi's presence in it. Given what I
had just witnessed I suppose it was understandable. As my
head sank into the pillow, my last waking thoughts were
of Sarah Hammond. Such a pitiful creature she was who,
unlike myself, would find neither rest nor serenity in sleep
in this or any other night. How very sad it all was.

FIVE

When Is a Ghost Not a Ghost?

BREAKFAST CONSISTED OF the most marvelous spinach casserole. Croutons, pressed into the spinach, encircled it, while a layer of poached eggs, staring up at me like so many yellow suns, covered its top. I had two slices.

"Seems odd, like," announced Vi as she skewered a bit of egg onto her fork, "to be eating breakfast at this hour. Why, it's nearly noon."

"After being up half the night, I daresay we won't be the only ones to be eating late," I answered. For we, as had the others, by the look of the empty tables around us, had slept well past the usual hour of rising.

"Aye," she replied. "No doubt it won't be too long before the rest of 'em starts straggling in. But 'ere, Em," she continued, as I set about refilling our empty cups from the last of the potted tea, "go on with what you were telling me about seeing Sarah, and all."

"There's not much more I can say, really," I answered. "Other than what I've already told you upstairs. Horrifying at the time, yes, but, looking back on it in the cool clear

71

light of morning, I'd also have to say it was the most fascinating moment in my life.''

"Fascinating!'' exclaimed my companion. ''That's not the word you'd catch me using to describe how I felt when I saw the captain floating down the hall.''

"Floating now, was he?'' I queried with a faintly bemused smile.

"Well,'' she hedged, ''he may not have actually been floating. But,'' she added, this time a little more defensively, ''that's not to say he couldn't have if he'd a mind to. Right?''

"Mmmm,'' I murmured. A noncommittal response but at least it had the effect of satisfying her.

"And,'' she continued, ''speaking of ghosts and whatnot, I think there's summat you should know 'bout this 'ere Sarah Hammond.''

"Something I should know?''

"Aye. I didn't make mention of it before, thinking how it might upset you like. But now that you've seen her and all, to my way of thinking it were her what moved your sachet packet from dresser top to drawer.''

"Why, Violet Warner!'' I exclaimed. ''Those were my thoughts exactly. I said nothing to you for the very same reason.''

"Quite the pair, ain't we?'' she responded with a good-natured chuckle.

"What's that old saying?'' I asked. ''Great minds think— Oh, the Christies.''

"The Christies?'' repeated Vi with a look of puzzlement. ''What about 'em?''

"They just walked in,'' I answered. With Vi facing me with her back to the open dining room door, I had the advantage of first seeing all who entered.

Mr. Christie was a well-proportioned man (though probably a little heavier than he should have been for a man of his height), with eyes that seemed to be continually darting about like a bird looking for someplace to land. The red-veined nose that sat between those eyes was an indication to me the man was no stranger to spirits. Bottled, mind, not ethereal. His wife I found to be pretty enough, though as she walked by it was all I could do not to be repelled by her cheap perfume that seemed to permeate the air. As to her yellow-checkered dress, it was, in my opinion, a little too gaudy for my taste. But then again, if I had been a good thirty years younger might not I have chosen it for myself as well? The dress I could forgive. But the perfume? Never.

I received an obligatory nod of greeting from the couple as they crossed in front of us and settled themselves down at their table. As it was but one away from ours and, never before having had the opportunity of speaking to them directly, I now took the initiative by offering up a good morning. They in turn responded in kind, and the ice, as they say, was broken.

"Terrible thing, that," announced Mr. Christie after introductions had been exchanged all round. "I mean, about Mr. Latham dying the way he did up in the attic." I must have looked surprised at his knowledge of it for he added that Mr. Burbage had approached them with the news just before their entering the room for breakfast.

"You could have knocked us over with a feather when we heard about it. Ain't that right, Bill?" spoke Mrs. Christie. Her husband nodded in agreement.

"And you slept through all that ruckus that was going on last night, did you?" questioned Vi.

"I'll be straight with you, Mrs. Warner, and you too, Mrs. Hudson," replied the man. "I'll tell you the same as what I told Mr. Burbage no more than five minutes ago."

"And what would that be, Mr. Christie?" I asked.

"That Liza and I did hear something going on, right enough. By that I mean," he added, "we could hear voices out in the hall. 'Bout two o'clock in the morning it was."

"No doubt," I replied, "that would have been both Mrs. Warner and myself as well as Mr. Burbage."

"And later like," he continued, "we could hear the sound of feet tramping up and down the attic stairs."

"That'd be the police," announced Vi.

"Yes, well, like I say, we know that now from what Mr. Burbage told us."

"Were neither of you curious enough last night," I asked, "to venture out of your room for a look-see?"

"Oh, me and Bill were, like you say, curious enough, Mrs. Hudson," spoke Liza Christie. "But after what we had gone through a few hours earlier that night—well, you tell 'em, luv."

Vi and I immediately focused our attention on Mr. Christie who appeared all too eager to tell the tale.

"Thinking my whistle needed a bit of a wetting, so to speak," he began, "I decided to take myself down to the local pub. What time would that have been, Liza, me luv?"

" 'Bout nine-thirty, no more than," she answered.

"Right. What with cutoff time being ten sharp, I figured I'd still have time to down a brew or two. So, with a quick kiss and a cheerio to the wife I flings open our door and, when I do, I near faints dead away."

"You saw him!" exclaimed Vi.

"Saw him I did, Mrs. Warner," he readily confirmed. "Captain Hammond it was and no mistake. Why, I could have reached out and touched him, he were that close. 'Course," he added, "at the time that was the last thing I wanted to do."

"Well, I should say!" voiced my companion most heartily.

"Did he approach you at all?" I asked. "Or make any menacing gestures?"

"Approach me? No, nor do I know what I would have done if he had," he confessed. "But as for, as you say, menacing gestures," he went on, "his eyes fair burned into mine, something fierce, they did. And he had what I'd call a wicked sneer on his face."

"An evil spirit, that's what he is," stated Vi very knowingly to one and all.

"Tell the ladies what happened next, Bill," urged his wife.

Her husband obliged by informing us the captain then

raised his one good arm above his head, which Mr. Christie illustrated by raising his own left arm in like fashion, stating that it was at this point that the ghostly figure ascended upward toward the ceiling where it subsequently disappeared.

"You see, Em," announced an all too smug Violet. "I told you he could float if he'd a mind to."

"What with him having disappeared and all," continued Mr. Christie, "I pops back into the room, locks the door, and there we stay for the rest of the night."

I then questioned him as to whether he had informed Mr. Burbage of his encounter with the captain and he answered that he had.

"Told him then, did you?" spoke Vi. "Doubt if the clock will strike another hour 'fore everyone in the bloomin' house has heard about it."

That being said, I watched as the man, in a show of exasperation, began to fidget about in his chair. This was followed by an incessant and annoying drumming of his fingertips to tabletop.

"I'm not one to complain, mind," he announced at last. "But a bit of food wouldn't go amiss right about now. Just listen to it rumble," he grumbled with a pat to his stomach. "Where *is* that woman?"

"Mrs. Burbage? I'm afraid," I answered, "what with last night and all, everyone is a bit off their schedule. From what she was saying earlier, even the cook showed up late for work this morning."

"Think they'd have more help, wouldn't you?" announced Liza Christie to no one in particular.

"From what I understand," I replied, "they won't be taking on extra staff 'til the first of June."

"Well, I hope they don't expect us to sit here 'til then," growled the man. "Could eat a horse, I could."

"A horse, is it?" commented Vi. "Oh, well, you're out of luck there, m'lad. "All you'll get here is spinach casserole."

Her quip produced a round of laughter. "And are you

two fellow Londoners as well?" I asked when the laughter had subsided.

"Londoners, yes, that's right," he answered. "First time down here for the both of us. Closed up shop and headed down here for a bit of a holiday, we did, Liza and me."

"Oh, yes? And what kind of shop would that be then, Mr. Christie?" asked Vi.

"Fish and chips, Mrs. Warner," he announced. "The best you ever tasted if I do say so myself. There'll be a couple of plates of 'em for you two ladies whenever you're in the neighborhood. On the house, so to speak."

"Oh, lovely," gushed Vi. "Whereabouts are you then?"

"On the Strand," he replied.

"Why," I said, "we're not all that far from there. Whereabouts on the Strand?"

"Yes, well," he answered, "it's not actually on the Strand, as such. It's on a little street what runs off it. Mews Lane."

"Mews Lane?" I repeated. "It doesn't ring a bell. Vi?"

"Sounds familiar," she said. "But never mind, we'll find it quick enough seeing as how it's a free meal and all."

"Seen anything of Brighton since you've been here?" Mrs. Christie asked of me.

"No, not really," I said. "We're down here for a bit of a rest rather than to go gallivanting about. Though Mrs. Warner did manage a bit of a trip into town with the Trefanns the other day."

"Problem is," said Vi, "the weather hasn't been all that cheerful, has it? Give my good right arm, I would," she added, "for a few good days of sunshine."

"You should at least visit the piers," the woman advised us. "Especially at night when they turn all the lights on. All lit up like a million Christmas trees, they are. Ain't that right, Bill?"

"Now's the best time to see it," stated her husband. "During the summer it's all you can do to get near the place. Why, they've had over ten thousand people down there on a single day, all milling and gawking about. But like the wife says, it's something to see."

"I don't know about going down tonight," I replied, as Vi and I arose from our table. "But perhaps we will later on this afternoon if Mrs. Warner and I are feeling up to it. Ah," I added with a smile on seeing a harried Mrs. Burbage enter with a trayful of food, "it seems your breakfast has arrived at last. Enjoy."

As it was, Vi and I did take ourselves out for the afternoon. And a very enjoyable one it turned out to be. At the four-corner junction where West Street meets Queens Road along with two others whose names I can't remember (though I believe it was North Street and Western Road) we came upon a clock tower built in commemoration of Her Majesty's 1887 Jubilee. I found its classical baroque style rather pleasing. However, with Vi expressing little interest in it, we pressed onward. Our journey eventually led us past the Theatre Royal on New Road where, if memory serves me right, they were presenting the comedy *Charlie's Aunt*. Vi and I immediately made plans to see it before our return trip home. But on coming upon the Empire and seeing it was a music hall featuring Lillie Langtry for the next three days, Vi just as quickly changed her mind regarding the Royal.

"Oh, I'd love to see her, I would," she said, on noting a hesitancy on my part. "Quite the entertainer she is, they say. Call her the Jersey Lily, they do," she announced very knowingly.

"But Vi," I reasoned, "we could have seen her any number of times when she was appearing in London."

"Aye, that may be as is. But," she added, "you do things on holidays you don't do at home." Thereby ending all further discussion on the subject.

Having strolled the promenade, taken in the marvelous steel-structured piers that stretched out over the ocean, and visited the overwhelming number of shops that lay in wait for tourists such as we, it was little wonder that we now found ourselves completely exhausted.

"If the shopkeepers relied on the likes of us for a living," announced Vi as we settled ourselves on a nearby park bench, "they'd be hard-pressed not to end up in the poorhouse. Didn't buy a thing, really. 'Cept this 'ere toffee. Want a chunk?" she asked, extending the bag of sweets.

I shook my head no, and delved into my handbag. "Here," I said, withdrawing my package, "a little something for you. A hand-knitted shawl. I bought it when you were in the shop buying your sweets."

"What? For me? Well, that were right nice of you, Emma," she announced with a wide smile. "Thanks ever so. I'd best wait 'til we gets back 'fore opening it."

"I hope you like it," I said.

"Well, if I don't," she replied with a playful nudge, "we could always give it to Sarah,"

"Oh, Vi, really," I clucked disapprovingly, though not without a wry smile. For here along a sunlit shore with fresh breezes playfully whipping the brims of our hats, and surrounded by people bent on nothing but pleasure, the spectral shadows of Burbage House seemed, at best, no more than a bad dream. "By the way," I added, "what on earth do you intend to do with all those seashells you collected along the beach earlier this afternoon?"

"Why," she answered with a pat to her pocketed shells, "I had an idea of making a present of them to Doctor Watson. As a souvenir like, from Brighton. He'll be ever so pleased, I'm sure," she added, without, thankfully enough, asking me to voice my opinion on the gift one way or the other.

By now the sun, no doubt believing it had done its duty by having shown itself for the better part of the day, had taken leave of us behind a billowing mass of clouds edged in threatening grey. I shivered slightly at this turnabout in the weather and suggested we call it a day. Vi readily agreed.

Leaving the bench behind for other tired souls with equally tired feet, we began our walk back whilst all the while keeping an eye out for an empty cab. " 'Ere, that's odd," announced Vi after we had gone but a short distance.

"What is?"

"Over there, that shop," she said, pointing a finger in the direction of her gaze. "Where it says 'Christie's Fish and Chips.' Thought he told us he were from London.''

"That doesn't mean it's the same Christie," I said, adding that it was a common enough name.

"Aye. True enough, I suppose. Still," she remarked, while continuing to take in the shop from our vantage point across the street, "it makes one wonder, don't it?"

"No, not really," I answered in all honesty. "But seeing there are no cabs about and, having nothing better to do 'til one comes along, we could pop over there to check it out if that's what you wish." I hadn't really expected her to agree, but she did, and we took off across the street.

A tinkling bell set above the door signaled our entrance into a shop I found to be a little worse for wear than most. On one side of a plaster-cracked wall a portrait of a grim-faced Queen Victoria gazed down on us, somewhat disdainfully, I thought. The three or four spindle-legged tables and chairs that sat along the wall remained unoccupied. The only customer, as such, being one small boy who, after paying for his cone-shaped newspaper filled to overflowing with salt-and-vinegared chips, beat a hasty retreat out the door. With the lad's departure we were left alone with a big, muscular man behind the counter who was busily engaged in flipping white, finger-size potatoes about in his wire basket. With his back toward us he gave it one last flip before resetting the basket into a vat of hot, bubbling oil.

"What'll it be, ladies?" he asked, turning round to give us his full attention as he did. "I've some nice fresh halibut what's just come in."

He stood before us wearing a grease-stained apron, a half-buttoned shirt, and a grimy neckerchief that served to absorb the sweat from his bull-thick neck. This was definitely not our Mr. Christie. Nor was I surprised to find that it wasn't. If Vi was disappointed, she made no mention of it. Her only response being that a cone full of chips might be nice. "Seeing that we're 'ere and all."

"Right you are then," replied the man. "Just give 'em a minute or two to golden," he added, with another shake of the basket.

"You're Mr. Christie then, are you?" I asked.

The sweat-beaded face broke into a grin. "Who, me? I'd like to say I was. No," he said, "I just work for the man. But if it's Mr. Christie you're looking for, you'll not find him here."

"Oh? And why is that?"

"He only shows up every so often. Just to see," he added with a wink, "that I haven't burned the place down."

"And this Mr. Christie you speak of," I continued, "would be a young man, would he? By that I mean somewhere in his thirties?"

"In his thirties!" he exclaimed. "Why, old Mr. Christie must be seventy if he's a day. And ailing, too. Only makes it down here whenever he's feeling up to it. But I could make mention you were looking for him next time he shows up, Mrs.—ah?"

"No, no, that's quite all right," I replied, feeling a little foolish. "It seems we're talking about two different Mr. Christies." With that, the matter was dropped. When Vi at last had her chips, I thanked the man for his time and off we went. Once outside the shop I turned on my companion and, in no little annoyance, announced what a waste of time it all had been.

"Well," she answered somewhat indifferently, in between a mouthful of chips, "we had it to waste, didn't we?"

"Why in the world," I continued, "you thought our Mr. Christie had some sort of secret fish and chip shop here in Brighton, I'll never know. That's about the silliest thing we've ever done."

"Say what you like," she countered, "but it weren't all for naught. The chips are good."

"Which is probably the reason," I shot back, "why you wanted to go in there in the first place."

"Oh," she said, ignoring my rebuttal, "there's one."

"One? One what?"

"A hansom," she answered. "Hoy, cabbie!"

On our arrival back at Burbage House I went directly to our room and plopped myself down on the side of the bed. Vi entered a few minutes later with a basin of warm water she had procured from Mrs. Burbage in which to soak our aching feet. Having done so and, with each feeling the better for it, we changed for dinner and headed downstairs.

After dinner, we, as did the others, drifted into the reading room where the buzzing conversation centered around the aforementioned Mr. Christie and his encounter the previous night with the vaporous Captain Hammond. The guests' knowledge of it no doubt having come by way of the garrulous Mr. Burbage. It appeared the demise of Mr. Latham was now secondary as a topic of discussion. As for Mr. Christie, he seemed only too willing to regale one and all with his tale.

Not to be outdone, Mr. Trefann, as did Vi, stepped forward to once again recount their own particular sighting of the captain. Each of them, I noted with some amusement, as had Mr. Christie, embellished their story far beyond the original telling of it. Fortunately, I had a chance to draw my companion aside to request she refrain from all mention of my having seen Sarah Hammond. This I would keep to myself. It was a far too personal experience. And one that I could not find within myself to share so easily with others.

"So, that's the pair of them, is it?"

"What?" I turned round to find Mr. Jones standing just to the back of me, taking in the Hammond portrait on the far wall. "Oh, yes, it is," I answered. "You've not seen the painting before, Mr. Jones?"

"No, I don't believe so," he replied. "If I had, I didn't make the connection 'til now."

"Seems we can't escape them," I remarked with a smile.

"Although," I added, "it would appear, young sir, that you and I are the only ones not to have had an encounter with the captain."

"And thankful I am for that, Mrs. Hudson, for I'm still of the opinion that the seeing of him was the cause of Mr. Latham's death."

"Mmmm. Oh, by the way," I said, "there's something I've been meaning to ask you. About that letter to your wife, did you—?"

"Got it off first thing this morning," he quickly replied. "And if she does take to heart what I wrote and comes down, we'll still have a few good days together here. Do you think she'll come, Mrs. Hudson?"

I assured him most wholeheartedly I was of the opinion that indeed she would. Actually, I may have laid it on a bit thick, but he seemed to be slowly coming out of his funk and I had no wish to see the poor man sink back into it. And with a few added words of encouragement and a pause for one last look at the painting (it still puzzled me for some reason), I excused myself from his presence and drifted off toward my companion. Seeing her engaged in chitchat with Mrs. Trefann, I interrupted their conversation just long enough to mention to Vi I was heading back up to our room. She answered she'd be along shortly, and off I went.

It was a good half hour later before she finally returned. "At last!" I sang out, before she had even closed the door behind her.

" 'Ere, what's all this 'at last' business, eh?" she quizzed in a show of bemused annoyance. "I'm on some sort of curfew now, am I?"

"No, no, nothing like that," I laughed. "It's about all this ghost business," I added in a rush of words. "I couldn't wait 'til you got back to tell you. I think I've—"

"What? Seen the captain?"

"No," I answered. "Nothing like that. But perhaps," I added, in a play on words, "I've seen through him."

"Eh?"

"To be honest with you, Vi," I confessed, "I never did

fully accept the fact that what we have walking the halls or poking about in the attic is the spiritual body of the late Captain Hammond.''

"What's this you're saying?" she exclaimed. "What with me having seen him, as well as others I could mention? Doubt if you'd be of a mind to think that if you'd come upon him yourself, Emma Hudson.''

"Hear me out, Vi," I implored. "It suddenly came to me, as I sat here waiting for you, what it was that was puzzling me about this whole affair. Actually, it was something I remembered you saying earlier this morning that made it all click into place.''

"Oh, aye, summat I said, was it?" was the skeptical response. "And what would that have been then?''

"You mentioned something about giving your good right arm for a few days of sunshine—or words to that effect.''

"Why," she replied, giving me the oddest look, "that's just an expression, that is. It doesn't mean—''

"No, no," I interrupted. "You don't understand. The point is, you said your good *right* arm." From the look on her face I could see I'd left her completely befuddled. And no wonder. My thoughts were tumbling out in words of no particular order. This wouldn't do. I collected myself by taking a deep breath and began again on a different tack. "I think I can best explain it this way," I said. "We'll pretend it's the night you say you saw the captain's ghost. You've just stepped from loo to hallway, right?''

"Aye, right enough, I suppose," she agreed, albeit somewhat belligerently. "But you'll not convince me that—''

"Now, hold on," I urged. "Just play along with me. Stand right about where you are now, as if you'd just come out into the hall. Good. Now then, I'll be the captain. I'll stand here in front with my back to you. There, is that the way it was?" I asked, on taking my position.

"Not really," she answered. "He were way up the hall.''

"Yes, Vi, I understand," I replied, trying not to show my annoyance. "But we'll have to make do with what room we have, won't we? Right. Now, you said," I continued, "he paused and turned slightly as if aware he was being watched. Which way?"

"Which way what?"

"Oh, Vi. Which way did he turn?"

"Why, to the left, it was."

I turned in that direction. "And is this when you saw he had but one arm?"

"Aye, that's right," she answered. "From what light there was, I could see his empty sleeve tucked into his coat pocket."

"Which arm would that have been?"

"Why, the left one, of course," she stated, clearly annoyed by the question.

"But my dear Mrs. Warner," I informed her, with a well-satisfied smile, "it was the right arm the captain had amputated, not the left."

"Who says?" she shot back.

"The painting," I announced. "The portrait of the Hammonds clearly shows it to be the captain's right arm that's missing. Not the left. With the couple having actually sat for the portrait," I added, "the artist himself could hardly have made such a blunder."

Vi shook her head in exasperated confusion. "Right arm, left arm," she fumed. "What's it all mean anyway, eh?"

"What it means," I answered, "is that we have someone pretending to be the ghost of Captain John Hammond. Someone who made the error of tucking the wrong sleeve into the captain's coat—or a coat very much like it."

"Only one thing wrong with that," she replied. "There's not a man here what's only got one arm."

Oh, dear, she still hadn't got it. I explained that it's an easy enough trick to keep one's arm hidden within the coat while the sleeve itself hangs empty. From the look on her face I could see she still needed more convincing. "There's also the matter," I continued, "of his pausing when he thought he was being watched."

"He was," she said. "By me."

"Yes, but think about it, Vi," I replied. "Wouldn't you

say that's a human reaction, rather than a ghostly one?''

"But he disappeared," she countered. "How do you explain that?"

"As I remember you telling me," I answered, "you closed your eyes when first spotting him. As he was at the end of the hall where it turns to the left, he simply rounded the corner. You opened your eyes and he was gone."

"But," she pressed, "others saw him, same as me."

"One of them is lying," I answered.

"The one who's pretending to be the ghost, is that it?"

"Exactly."

"It's a queer business, this," she stated with a rueful shake of her head. "I mean, why would anyone go gallivanting about the place dressed up like the captain? That's what I'd like to know."

"As would I, Mrs. Warner," I replied. "As would I."

SIX

The Star of Hyderabad

"LOOK, THERE'S AN empty table," sang out Vi as we entered one of Brighton's many restaurants the following day. "And by a window, too. I always like a table by the window, I do," she continued, after we had settled ourselves down and placed our order. "Gives us a chance while we're having our tea to see what's going on outside. 'Sides that," she added, "it's nice to get away from Burbage House for a change."

"Physically, at least," I answered, "if not mentally. My mind's still awhirl with a million questions."

"I don't know about a million," she replied, "but I do have one or two. Like, what about Mrs. Hammond, eh? Still think she's a spirit, do you?"

"Sarah? Oh, yes," I answered, as the memory of that sad and sallow face flashed through my mind. "I believe Sarah Hammond is truly a pathetic figure from the past who remains, tragically enough, unaware of being trapped between two worlds."

"Strange, though, ain't it, Em," spoke Violet after a thoughtful pause. "I were always taught that when you die you go straight to heaven. That is," she added, "if you've been good. But with this ghost business and all, seems to me it's a mite more complicated than that. Oh, lovely," she said, breaking off her train of thought on seeing the waitress approach with our tray. "Looks good enough to drink," she joked as the tea was set before us.

I wonder how many times the poor woman's heard that, I thought. "Oh, look," I announced with an eye toward the window. "Out there. Walking this way. Isn't that Inspector Radcliffe?"

Vi craned her neck and peered out. "Aye," she answered, "it's him, all right. Who's that with him?"

"Isn't that his sergeant? Oh, what's his name?"

"Styles?"

"Yes, that's right." As they were now opposite us on the other side of the glass, I tapped two or three times on the window. Both men stopped, smiled in recognition, and waved. I beckoned them in.

"And how are you two ladies enjoying your stay in Brighton so far?" asked the inspector as he and his sergeant took their places in the two remaining chairs at our table.

"I'd have to think twice 'fore answering that," replied Vi. "What with our finding poor Mr. Latham dead in the attic and ghosts running round willy-nilly like, I'd be hard-put to say it's been enjoyable."

The inspector seemed surprised and rather amused by her reply. "I say," he said, scarcely hiding a smile, "you two aren't still of the opinion that Latham's death was ghost-related, are you?"

"I am of the opinion, Inspector," I replied, "that yes, a spiritual entity does walk the halls of Burbage House. But," I added, "as to Brighton itself, I think I can speak for Mrs. Warner as well as myself when I say that we find it simply delightful."

"Far cry from the hurly-burly of London, eh?" he replied. As to spiritual entities, he made no further mention. Which I suppose was just as well.

"Indeed it is," I said. At this point, a void in the conversation was filled by the reappearance of our waitress.

"Pardon me, Mrs. Hudson," spoke the sergeant, after ordering tea for both himself and his superior. "I may be wrong, but didn't your name pop up once or twice in the papers in connection with the Bramwell murder in London a while back? I say that," he continued, "in remembering you speaking the other night of being engaged in criminal investigations from time to time."

"Why, I should say it did!" exclaimed Vi, before I had a chance to respond. "But then, only a line or two. You'd have never known it was Mrs. Hudson here what solved the case. With," she added in an aside, "an assist from me, if truth be known. 'Course, I can't really blame them—the newspapers, I mean. You can thank Mrs. Hudson herself for that, Sergeant. Likes to keep in the background, our Emma does."

"Speaking of investigations," I said, stepping in if for no other reason than to shift the focus of the conversation away from myself, "from the story as told to us by our venerable host, was it not you, Inspector, who was in charge of some sort of robbery that had taken place at Burbage's a few years back?"

"I know only too well the one of which you speak, Mrs. Hudson," he stated all too eagerly, with eyes lighting up in the memory of it. "A good ten years ago it was. But no, the late Inspector Grimes was in charge then. I was but a mere sergeant at the time. Oh, sorry, Styles," he added as an afterthought to his subordinate. "But, as I say," he went on, "I remember only too well working with Grimes on it. Quite the important case it was. I'd be safe in saying we've had nothing quite like it before or since. Whatever crime we do have here," he continued, "consists of nabbing the odd pickpocket or two down at the piers or along the promenade. But as to the robbery itself, if you ladies have the time—"

"All the time in the world," I answered.

"Always like to hear a good story, we do," added Vi.

"Unfortunately," he informed us, "I can't promise you

a happy ending. But we did catch the begger who did it.''

''What's this?'' quizzed Vi. ''I should think if you caught him, then that'd be an end to it.''

''Hear me out, Mrs. Warner,'' he replied. ''To begin at the beginning, Inspector Grimes and myself were on our way to investigate a robbery that had taken place at the old Windermere estate.''

''The home of Lord and Lady Ashcroft,'' announced his sergeant. ''Just outside of Brighton. And quite posh it is, too. I've never been inside it myself, mind, but they say it has over seventy rooms. And the gardens—''

''Yes, thank you very much, Styles,'' the inspector cut in through gritted teeth. ''We'll save the tour for another day, shall we? On our arrival,'' he began again, ''we were informed by a highly distraught Lady Ashcroft that her ring had been stolen from her private quarters.''

''That would be her bedroom,'' stated the sergeant.

''Yes, Styles, that would be her bedroom,'' repeated the visibly annoyed inspector. ''It seems,'' he continued, ''that on the previous evening when their lord and ladyship arrived home after having had attended some such ball or other, Lady Ashcroft, on returning to her room and being rather fatigued by the lateness of the hour, placed the ring on her dresser. Without bothering,'' he added, ''to lock it in her private safe. From what Lord Ashcroft told us, this was not the first time she had been so careless.''

''Seems to me,'' said Vi, ''that they were making a big to-do about a ring. Nice as though it may be, I'm sure.''

''Ah, but Mrs. Warner,'' spoke the inspector, ''this was no ordinary ring. Far from it, dear lady. For the setting contained the legendary Star of Hyderabad itself. A gem so beautifully cut and of such an immense size, one could scarcely put a price on it.''

His story was interrupted by the arrival of their tea. Thankfully, Sergeant Styles did not offer up his opinion that it looked good enough to drink. The inspector continued his story.

''I therefore thought myself quite fortunate,'' he said,

"when, under my intense questioning of the household staff, Lady Ashcroft's upstairs maid broke down and admitted her part in the theft. Her gentleman friend, she confessed, was the actual thief. She had, she said, merely left a window conveniently open for him. As for her gentleman friend, it seems he was none other than a certain night burglar from around these parts by the name of Charlie Allbright. And well known to us he was too, with a record as long as your arm. According to the maid, Annie," he continued, pausing only for a sip of his tea, "after things had cooled down a bit, the plan was for her to meet him in two days' time at Burbage's, where he'd taken a room. From there, the two of them would hightail it to London where Allbright had a buyer for the gem."

"But it's you and Inspector Grimes who arrived at Burbage's instead of Annie," I said.

"True enough," he replied, breaking into a grin. "Bit of a shock for old Charlie boy, that was."

"And what of the gem? This Star of Hyderabad?" I asked.

"I'm sorry to say we never recovered it. The way I see it," he added, "Allbright was tipped off somehow that we were on our way over to pick him up and disposed of it just before we arrived."

"Disposed of it?" I queried. "How d'you mean?"

"It's my theory, Mrs. Hudson," he answered, "that there was a second man involved in the theft. If I'm right, it was this second man he passed the diamond ring along to. Realizing that when we arrived we'd have no case against him if the gem wasn't found to be in his possession. Unfortunately for Charlie," he went on, as Vi and I continued to sit in rapt attention, "in our search of his room we came across a brooch, later to be indentified as belonging to Lady Ashcroft, that he also nicked that same night. We learned later that he had planned on giving it to the maid Annie."

"And her confessing he was the thief first chance she got," announced Vi. "Just goes to show you."

"And it was just that confession of hers, Mrs. Warner,"

continued the inspector, "along with the finding of the brooch that sent Charlie boy away for a good long time."

"And where had the brooch been hidden?" I asked.

"Whether it had been hidden or whether it had slipped his mind in his haste to transfer the diamond to his partner in crime, I don't know. But as to its location," he informed me, "I found it lodged in the back of his dresser drawer. And oh, didn't that put Grimes's nose out of joint—what with it being me who found it," he chuckled.

"And you being but a mere sergeant at the time," commented Styles, oh, so innocently.

The inspector was not amused.

"What about this 'ere maid, Annie?" asked Vi, stepping in at just the right moment. "Whatever happened to her, eh?"

"Annie Potter? She received a much lighter sentence than did her gentleman friend," replied the inspector. "On her release from prison she was, as far as I know, never seen or heard from again."

"And as to this Charlie Allbright," I queried, "still in custody, is he?"

"Charlie? Dead, Mrs. Hudson. Died in his prison cell over three years ago. Heart attack, I believe it was."

"And he never revealed what happened to the gem? Or," I added, "whether there had indeed been another man involved in the theft?"

"I'm afraid not, Mrs. Hudson. No deathbed confession, if that's what you mean. Styles here," he added, with but a brief glance at the man opposite him, "was actually with him at the time of his death, as I recall."

"Indeed I was, Inspector," confirmed the sergeant. "I was a constable at the time, Mrs. Hudson, and—"

"And could be again," muttered his superior, before downing the last of his tea.

"And," continued Styles, choosing to ignore the barbed remark, "working the prison night shift on the very evening he died. I remember rushing down to his cell on hearing Eddie call out for help."

"Eddie?"

"Eddie Dobbs—his cell mate, Mrs. Hudson," he answered. "When I got there I could see Charlie lying on his cot, his face white as new snow, with Eddie bending over him. I unlocked the cell door and, with nightstick in hand—just in case they were trying to pull a fast one—I entered. As I did, I heard Charlie gasping out to his mate the words—or at least what sounded like the words—'Haddock, Eddie, haddock.' Then the old ticker just gave out on him. 'Course, it made no sense—the words, I mean. His mind must have been wandering, like as not."

"Perhaps," offered Vi, "he were thinking of fish. They say you think of all sorts of queer things just before you pass on."

"Fish? Oh, yes, a haddock, I see what you mean," replied the inspector, as the two men exchanged a smile. "Well, whatever it meant, if anything," he carried on, "it has nothing to do with the missing gem. Which, in all likelihood," he added, "would have by now been cut down into smaller stones. I doubt very much if it was left as is."

"Why's that then?" asked Vi. I wondered myself.

"A gem as famous as the Star of Hyderabad," he informed us, "could never be displayed publicly without the entire diamond industry being made aware of its presence."

We nodded in understanding. I then thought to ask, out of curiosity if for no other reason, what he could tell us of this Eddie Dobbs person.

"Confidence man," he answered. "That was Eddie Dobbs. Sell you the Tower of London, he would, and you'd be none the wiser for it."

"Odd, his name coming up now," interjected Styles.

"Oh? And why is that?" I asked.

"What the sergeant is no doubt referring to, Mrs. Hudson," replied the inspector, regaining the conversational lead, "is the fact that Dobbs, after having been discharged from prison no more than a fortnight ago, was found beaten to death less than two days after his release."

"Oh, how terrible."

"But not surprising," added the sergeant. "What with the kind of life his lot leads."

"And who was it, Inspector," teased Vi, "that said summat about pickpockets being the only crime worth mentioning around 'ere?"

"An ex-convict found dead after having engaged in a drunken brawl behind a pub," replied the unflappable Inspector Radcliffe, "hardly constitutes a crime wave, Mrs. Warner."

"And have you no clue as to who it was that brought about his death?" I asked.

"What we do know—oh, by the way, would you ladies care for more tea? Now, where was I?" he asked, after Vi and I had declined his offer with thanks. "Oh, yes—what we do know," he began again, "is that Dobbs was last seen drinking and chatting it up with another man at one of the local watering holes before leaving with the man by way of the back entrance. Sometime after that, Dobbs was found in back of the privy behind the pub with his head bashed in. We found the rock that did him in but, unfortunately, not the man. At least," he added, "not yet."

"But surely, Inspector," I said, "it shouldn't be all that difficult. There must have been eyewitnesses who—"

"Eyewitnesses, is it!" he snorted. "Oh, yes, there were eyewitnesses, Mrs. Hudson. According to those we questioned, including the publican and his staff, the man we're looking for is either short, tall, fat, thin, bushy-bearded, or clean-shaven. Give me circumstantial evidence any day," he sighed. "If we had only to rely on so-called eyewitnesses—well, you see what I mean. And that, ma'am," he concluded, "is about all I can tell you."

I spoke for Vi as well as myself by acknowledging that we had found the story to have been most enlightening. That being said, the inspector, with a glance at the clock on the far wall, announced it was time he and Styles had best get a move on. As they arose from their chairs we again thanked them for their time as well as for a most enjoyable get-together. They reciprocated in kind, with the sergeant lingering for a moment beside our table as the inspector made his way to the door. "About this ghost business of yours," he whispered, with a furtive glance back at the retreating Radcliffe, "I'd pay no never-mind to what the inspector thinks. I had an aunt once who used to hold what they call séances in me mum's parlor. I was just a tyke at the time. But I can remember seeing—"

"Styles!" barked the inspector.

After having returned to Burbage's in time for dinner, which we enjoyed at a leisurely pace, we then retired to the reading room. Finding no one else present, I took the opportunity of bringing Vi face-to-face with the Hammonds' portrait. It took but a glance for my companion to see that it was indeed the right sleeve of the captain's coat that was devoid of any arm. To paraphrase, the proof was in the painting. As to the rest of the evening, whether it was Violet or myself who first spotted an old cribbage board alongside a well-thumbed deck of cards on the corner table, I don't know. In any event, on seeing it, we decided to opt for a game of cribbage as a way to while away an hour or two.

"Fifteen two, and a pair is four," announced a gleeful Violet on laying down her cards and, just as gleefully, pegging the winning hole. "That's three in a row I've won so far!" she exclaimed.

"Must be your lucky night," I answered.

"Either that," she said, casting a fish eye in my direction, "or someone I know isn't concentrating on their game the way they should be."

"You're right," I admitted, while in the process of making a halfhearted attempt at shuffling the cards. "I'm afraid my mind hasn't been on the game."

"Couldn't be you're thinking about getting involved in this 'ere Dobbs murder, could it?" she quizzed. "Why," she said, "I should think we've got enough to worry about as it is."

"True enough," I agreed, setting the cards aside. Thereby

signaling my intention of terminating the game. Vi, it
should be noted, voiced no objection. No doubt being of
the opinion it was better to quit now while she was still
ahead. "As to the idea of my launching an investigation
into the murder of Eddie Dobbs," I stated, "I think not.
That's the inspector's case. It has nothing to do with us.
No," I said, "it's this masquerade business that has me
stymied."

"You mean as to who it is that's pretending to be the
old sea captain?"

"Exactly. For pretending he is. The painting proves that.
Plus the fact that, according to the late Mr. Latham, there
had been no sighting of the captain for at least a good five
years. Yet his reappearance very nicely coincided with the
arrival of our fellow guests. And does he return to his usual
haunt? No," I announced. "This particular Captain Hammond extends his wanderings to hallway, attic, and who
knows where else?"

"Makes one wonder, don't it?"

"Not anymore it doesn't," I answered. "It's perfectly
obvious to me that one of the men in this house is a tourist
by day and a one-armed sea captain by night."

"And who's the big winner?"

The male voice suddenly booming up from behind set
Vi and I halfway out of our seats. "Why, Mr. Jones," I
exclaimed on turning round, "you near gave us both a heart
attack!"

"Oh, it's terrible sorry I am," he quickly apologized. "I
thought you saw me coming."

"Seems we were too caught up in our little chin-wag to
notice," added Vi, in trying to make the best of it.

"I just popped in for something to read," he said, holding a book aloft for all to see. "When I saw you over here,
I just—"

"No need to explain, Mr. Jones, we're no worse for
wear. As to the big winner," I answered, harking back to
his question, "I'm afraid it was Mrs. Warner. Not my night
it seems."

He sympathized, congratulated Vi, acknowledged he had little interest in either cards or cribbage, and, with not much else to say one way or the other, bade us both good night.

" 'Ere," spoke Vi on his departure, "do you think he heard anything of what we were saying?"

I shook my head. "I've no idea," I said. "But if he's not our captain, it won't matter if he did, will it?"

"And if he is?" she asked.

"That, Mrs. Warner," I answered, "is a question best left unanswered."

" 'Course," she added, "I'm not saying it's him, mind. Seems nice enough, he does. But if you ask me, if you want to get to the bottom of it, I say the next time we hear moving about from above, we should both hightail it up there. Catch whoever it is red-handed, as they say. What do you think?"

"I think," I replied, "you'd better think again."

"What's that supposed to mean?"

"Are you forgetting that was exactly what Mr. Latham did? And we know what happened to him."

"Well," she countered, "we could always wait in the hallway for him to come down."

"I shouldn't think we'd be in any less danger in the hallway than in the attic," I answered, noting Vi's exasperation. Not with me so much but to the situation as it stood. We seemed to be blocked at every step. She offered up one last suggestion which was that when hearing footsteps from above we should take to knocking on the doors of our fellow lodgers. The thought being, the man missing from his room would be our Captain Hammond. "A good idea," I replied in a complimentary fashion, before letting her down as easy as I could. "But," I added, "to go rapping on doors in the early hours of the morning wouldn't exactly endear us to those within, with nerves being as taut as they are already around here."

Her face sagged and her shoulders drooped. "Well," she said, offering up a sigh of despair, "I don't know what to do then."

"You're tired," I said. "As I am myself. Perhaps one of us will come up with another idea or two tomorrow, after a good night's sleep."

"A good night's sleep, you say?" she repeated with a scowl on rising from the table. "I haven't had a good night's sleep since we left Baker Street."

Having no reply, I left the cards and cribbage board as we had found them and followed Vi back up to our room. Whether the midnight hour found our mysterious lodger in the attic above our heads, I have no idea. For, thankfully enough, the two of us slept like logs (silly expression, that) until the first shaft of morning's light found its way into our room. And grateful we were for the uninterrupted sleep. For the following night would be quite a different matter.

SEVEN

Meet Me at Midnight

༄MORNING HAD DAWNED bright and cheerful. So much so that by mid-afternoon we had taken ourselves out onto the verandah to enjoy the loveliest May day since our arrival. With closed eyes I sat there letting the sun sweep over me while Vi maintained a steady back and forth movement on the verandah's solitary rocker. Would that all our time here could be as peaceful as this, I mused, with a contented sigh to myself.

"Thought any more about how we're going to get a fix on you know who?" asked Vi, and, by so asking, breaking my reverie.

I opened my eyes to announce that yes, I had been toying with an idea or two. But it was a small white lie, actually. For I still hadn't the foggiest idea on how to confront in the dead of night a man who, in the guise of another, had no doubt been responsible for the demise of Mr. Latham. If truth be told, I really hadn't given it much thought. For my mind this day had been on my late husband, William. Understandably, I suppose, since he and John Hammond had both been men of the sea. But unlike the captain, Wil-

liam's passage from this world to the next had been clear
sailing with but one last lingering sigh before his final departure. Unlike the ghosts of Burbage, no haunted spectre,
he. That, in itself, gave me comfort.

"Well, let's hear it then," said Vi.

"Hear it? Hear what?"

"You said you had an idea or two," she replied.

What now? I thought. I was saved from having to admit
my lie by the appearance of Mrs. Trefann, who stepped out
quite unexpectedly onto the verandah. "Oh, Mrs. Hudson,
Mrs. Warner, how nice to see you," she said, offering up
a smile on her approach. "Taking in the sun, are you?"

"Taking it in while we can," replied Vi.

I offered the woman a chair but she declined, stating that
she was in fact waiting for her husband. "I don't know
what's keeping him," she added with an eye toward the
door. "I thought he was right behind me."

"More'n likely," stated Vi, "he's bumped into Mr. Burbage. Talk your leg off, that one would."

She laughingly admitted that Vi might be right at that,
adding that perhaps she would sit down for a minute or two
after all.

"Off to see the sights then, are you, Mrs. Trefann?" I
asked as she settled herself down in the chair next to me.

"No," she answered, "nothing quite so ambitious as that
today. We thought—Harold and I, that is—that we'd take
in a bit of a stroll before lunch."

"I'm surprised your hubby would be wanting to head
out for a stroll," remarked Vi.

"Why do you say that, Mrs. Warner?"

"Well, I mean," explained Violet, "what with him being
a postman and all, seems going out for a walk is the last
thing he'd want to do."

"Oh, I see. No," she said, "Harold loves to walk. Which
is just as well, I suppose. Besides," she added, "he thought
it might do me some good."

"Been ailing, have you, Mrs. Trefann?" I asked.

"Not in the way you might think, Mrs. Hudson," she

replied. Realizing she couldn't leave it at that, she announced, albeit somewhat hesitantly, that she hadn't been feeling all that well since having had the horrifying experience of being confronted by the ghostly image of Sarah Hammond.

Her admission, needless to say, came as a complete and utter shock to both myself and Vi. Though why it did, I don't know. By now, I thought, we would have learned to expect the unexpected. But it seemed we were not quite so blasé about ghostly visitations as we would have liked to believe. "And when," I asked, being only too eager to hear all the details, "did this sighting of yours take place?"

"This very morning," she stated. "Which, in some way, seemed to make it all that more ghastly. I mean," she went on, "one usually thinks of that sort of thing happening on some dark and dreary windswept night. But to come across such an apparition during the daylight hours—" She shivered at whatever mental pictures were being played out in her mind.

"Where was it you saw her then?" asked Vi.

"You know that door at the end of the stairway wall? The one that leads into the kitchen?" We nodded that we did. "There," she said. "With my husband having left for breakfast a few minutes before, I was on my way downstairs to join him. But," she added, "as I reached the bottom step something—I don't know what it was—but something made me pause and turn my head in the direction of the door. As I did, I saw this . . . this image, if you want to call it that, of Sarah Hammond passing right through it. The door, mind!" she exclaimed. "Solid wood, it is. But, as I say, she passed through it as if it never existed."

I asked if the woman's spirit had spoken to her or had said anything during the encounter.

"Not a word," she answered. "I don't think she was even aware of my presence. Her head was bowed and her walk slow but steady. But wait," she added. "Yes, thinking back on it, she *was* saying something. One word, over and over again. But what that word was, I have no idea. It was more of a mumble than anything else. Then," she continued, "as she drew nearer to where I was standing, she began to . . . how would you say—evaporate? Yes, evaporate, before my very eyes, until nothing remained of that shadowy figure but my memory of her." Vi and I could do little but offer up our sympathy at what had undoubtedly been a most terrifying experience for her. "If Harold," she informed us, "hadn't come out of the dining room at that very minute to see what was keeping me, I would have fainted dead away. Don't know why I didn't in any case," she added with yet another shiver.

I then harkened back to her telling me of the word she had heard Mrs. Hammond repeating over and over again and asked whether that word could have been *John*.

"Why, yes," she said, turning to me with a look of amazement. "Now that you mention it, I believe it was. But," she questioned, "how on earth did you—?" She stopped, and her mouth dropped slightly open in the realization of the answer. "You've seen her too!" she exclaimed.

I answered that I had and offered up a brief version of my encounter. The fact that I had seen Sarah Hammond as well seemed to have a calming effect on her.

"Have you told anyone else about seeing her?" asked Vi. "The guests, or—?"

"Mrs. Burbage," she answered. "But," she said, "if I expected to get any sympathy from that woman I was sadly mistaken, I can tell you. Tried to laugh it off, she did. Said I had nothing to fear from the captain's wife and that I should look on her as one of the family. Can you imagine!"

"She's a luv, she is," was Vi's all too sarcastic reply. "Next thing you know she'll be setting out an extra plate for her at the dinner table."

"What with Harold having come upon the captain's ghost earlier and now with my seeing the spirit of his wife as well," confessed the woman, "I was all for leaving this morning. But my husband only has the one holiday a year and it would be a shame to cut it short. Oh, my," she added with a glance to the sky, "that sun *is* warm, isn't it? I don't think I'll need these." She set about removing her gloves and, after doing so, placed them on her lap.

I noticed she wore no wedding ring but said nothing lest the absence of it be a cause for embarrassment to her. Vi, it seemed, had made a similar observation and, with less compunction than I, made mention of the ringless finger.

"Oh, you noticed," was Mrs. Trefann's flustered response. "Yes, I suppose that's something women would notice, wouldn't they? Harold," she said, "has yet to see that it's missing. Thank goodness."

"You've lost it then, have you?" I asked with some concern.

"No, not really," she answered. "I've left it at home. Beside the kitchen sink, actually. I'd taken it off when doing the dishes then forgot all about it 'til we were halfway here on the train. Silly of me, I know."

" 'Ere, you're not the only one," Violet assured her. "I've done the same thing myself many a time, I have."

With the arrival of Mr. Trefann, who stepped out onto the verandah, his wife rose from her chair and, after Vi and I had had a word or two with the man, the couple set off on their walk. With their departure, I had expected my companion to further quiz me on how we were to find out who lurked within the attic. But with Mrs. Trefann's arrival and her telling of coming upon Sarah Hammond, it had obviously set her mind off in other channels of thought. I took advantage of the opportunity by tossing various schemes around in my mind throughout the better part of the day. And, by ten o'clock that night, as my companion was about to prepare herself for bed, I announced that I had at last formulated a plan.

Vi had set herself down on the side of the bed and was in the process of removing her shoes. "Well," she said, with a puff or two on bending over her raised knee, the better to grasp the laces, "out with it then."

"It might be best to leave those on," I said.

"What? Go to bed with me shoes on? 'Ere, hold on a

minute," she added with eyes narrowing in on me, "are you saying my shoes have summat to do with this 'ere plan of yours?"

"I should think you'd be in need of them," I answered. "Since the plan is to take ourselves up into the attic this very night."

"What! Go up in the attic?" she sputtered. "Why, Emma Hudson, if you recall, that were my idea. And you said—"

"And I said," I continued, "the danger would be too great if we were to suddenly jump out of the darkness to demand of our 'ghost' just what it is he's up to, or words to that effect."

"Well then?"

"The plan is," I informed her, "we do no such thing. Jump out, I mean. We enter before he arrives, conceal ourselves, and wait. There will be no confrontation. We will be there to secretly observe just who this so-called Captain Hammond really is. After he leaves," I informed her. "We take ourselves downstairs and return to our room. Simple enough, wouldn't you say?" Her reaction was to hem and haw before at last announcing that it all sounded a mite too risky. "Too risky?" I countered. "And who was it that wanted to spring upon him in the darkness?"

"Not one of my better ideas," she grudgingly admitted.

"You agree with my plan then?"

"I suppose. But I can't help but wonder what your William and my Albert would say if they could see all these 'ere shenanigans we get ourselves into."

"Perhaps they do see us," I answered. "As to what they might say," I added with a smile, "perhaps it's best if we don't know. In any case, I like to think of them as our guardian angels."

"Guardian angels, is it? Oh, yes," she said, "I can just see the two of them, I can, standing over us in their white robes, flapping their wings about. Coo!" she laughed. "What a sight."

Flapping wings or not, I was more than a little relieved

to have Vi go along with me. For I very much doubted if I'd go ahead with the plan on my own. After some further discussion we agreed among ourselves that the two of us would make our way up to the attic no later than eleven o'clock. This would ensure us plenty of time to find a suitable place to hunker down while we awaited the arrival of our supposed ghost. But if we were to ascend into the darkness above, a light was needed. And although our room was lit by gaslight, I did manage to find a tallow holder and a small candle in the back of one of the drawers. No doubt having been put there in case of emergency. And so it was that on the appointed hour, we set forth with candle in hand out the door.

"All we need now," remarked Vi, "is for someone to come out of the loo and see the pair of us tippy-toeing down the hall."

Fortunately, no one did and we arrived at our destination to find the attic door closed but, thankfully enough, devoid of any lock. Would not Mr. Latham be alive today, I wondered, if, in his role of handyman, he had taken the time to see that it had been properly secured? Then again, according to the Burbages, since it was naught but a ghost that roamed above, what need then for a lock? I couldn't help but think how it all seemed to work to the advantage of the man masquerading as Captain Hammond.

With Vi giving me a nudge to indicate we'd best get a move on, I began by very slowly opening the door and, thrusting the candle out before me, we proceeded by taking step by creaking step, ever upwards. With each creak and groan sounding (to our ears at least) louder than the one that preceded it, we afforded ourselves quiet sighs of relief on reaching the top. With a beam of moonlight through one small window to the back doing little to illuminate our surroundings, I swung the candle out in an arc and, as I did, Violet let out a gasp. "What? What is it?" I asked in a voice no more than a whisper.

"There's someone over there," she at last managed to

whisper back. "A woman. Just—just standing there, she is."

"A woman!" I repeated, scarcely believing what I heard. Then, for some reason, I immediately thought of Sarah Hammond. Wondering if her appearance boded ill for the two of us, I raised the flickering candle up so that its glow caught the outline of a female figure standing to the back of the attic. "I don't think *she'll* give us any trouble," I announced, somewhat amused and, I admit, more than a little relieved on realizing who it was that stood within the shadows. "It's a mannequin," I stated to a still somewhat uncertain Violet.

" 'Ere, you sure?"

"Quite. As a matter of fact, I had the pleasure of meeting her," I added with a smile in remembrance of my *faux pas*, "on the night we discovered Mr. Latham's body lying no more than a few feet away from where we now stand. Though as I remember," I continued, "on that night the mannequin was nearer to the stairs than what it is now."

"It's been moved then," she said. "Unless," she added with an impish grin, "it's been her what's been walking around up 'ere."

"Oh, it's been moved all right," I replied. "As have, no doubt, a good many other things as well."

"Aye," she agreed. "But what's all this 'pleasure of meeting her' business, eh?"

"Later, Vi," I said. "Right now, we'd best find ourselves a suitable place to hide in waiting for whoever it is that shows up."

"What happens if he don't?" she asked.

"The only thing we can do then," I replied with a resigned sigh, "would be to take ourselves up here every night until he does." As could be imagined, the idea of spending what few nights remained of our holiday hidden away in some attic was not something either one of us looked forward to. "I don't know why they didn't throw half of what's up here away in the first place," I remarked on looking round at the jumble of boxes, broken chairs, old furniture, and what have you. "What's the point in keeping it all anyway?"

"And when was the last time *you* were up in the attic on Baker Street, eh?"

I took her meaning and said no more in regard to over-filled attics.

"Oh, look over there, Em," she said, pointing to an oval-topped, three-legged table. "I wouldn't mind that for myself. Doesn't seem to be in too bad a condition."

"My dear Mrs. Warner," I announced, "this isn't an outing at some flea market we're on. Oh, look!" I exclaimed. "Now, *there's* something interesting."

"What! After telling me—"

"No, look," I said, turning the light in the direction of an old steamer trunk. "The markings on the catch where it's been pried away at are new." I opened the lid and peered round inside.

"See anything?" she asked.

"Nothing but a pile of musty, moth-eaten clothes," I replied, rummaging about before bringing forth a faded green satin dress from another era.

"Oh," said Vi, "that's nice. Or would have been when it was new. Do you think it could have belonged to Sarah?"

"I've no idea," I answered on setting it back in the trunk. "But the finding of it does lead one to speculate that it could have been this or some other trunk that contained a few items of the captain's apparel as well."

"It's the old sea captain's clothes that our ghost has taken to wearing, is that what you think?"

"I think," I replied, "that if we stand out here in the middle of the attic any longer, we'll have a chance to ask him in person. Come on," I said, "it's high time we found a spot to hunker down and wait." We began by making our way in and around a maze of paraphernalia, pausing only before the old sewing machine table for a silent thought or two before coming upon a china cabinet that was somewhat the worse for wear. "What do you think?" I asked.

"Oh," she said, "it's nice enough, mind. Though it could use a bit of fixing up. Look, you can see where the glass door has been cracked and—"

"No, Vi," I said. "I mean as a place to hide behind."

"Oh, I see. Well, I suppose. If you think we can squeeze in there."

On coming closer I could see what she meant by squeezing in. A number of cartons and boxes were piled up in back of it, affording us but a narrow passage in between cartons and cabinet in which to hide. "Well," I said, "let's give it a go, shall we?" After extinguishing the candle and setting it aside we at last managed to ease our way in. Once in back, we took advantage of one or two boxes on which to sit as best we could to await whatever the night might bring.

As we waited I began to be plagued by self-doubts. What if I'd been wrong? What if the noises heard in the night were truly made by a dead sea captain? What if—? No, I thought, it has to be someone as mortal as ourselves. The empty sleeve of the left arm, not the right, told me that much. But what if Vi had been wrong? From somewhere off in the distance a bell tolled the midnight hour.

Our vigil, which we maintained in a silence that would have done credit to a monk, was at last broken by Vi announcing, none too happily, that her left foot had fallen asleep. "Just as long as the rest of you doesn't," I quipped before adding that she should give it a good rub. Her reply was no more than a grumpy mumble. Whether directed at me or her foot, I had no idea, nor did I bother to ask. After a good half hour or so had gone by with neither sight nor sound of anyone entering the attic, I began to wonder if it had all been for naught.

"How are we going to see who it is if he does show up?" questioned Vi in some annoyance. No doubt becoming as tired of the game as I. "Barely see *you*, if it comes to that."

"Unless he has the eyes of a bat," I answered, "he'll have brought some sort of light along with him."

"A bat, you say? If you ask me, it's us what's the batty ones. Sitting 'ere all crunched up like two—"

"Shhh!"

"Eh?"

"Quiet!" I shot back, scarcely able to control my excitement. "There's someone coming!"

The heavy thud of feet to stair and the creaking it produced as they ascended, set both our hearts a-pounding. Frightened, yes, but being even more curious, I quietly eased myself up and poked my head out from the back of the cabinet just far enough to see flickers of light becoming that much brighter as he continued ever upward. "He'll be on the top step any second now," I whispered.

" 'Ere, let's have a look then," replied Vi, raising herself up from the boxed crate. I crouched down, the better for her to see over my head, and, with our moving about in what cramped quarters we had, I suddenly felt the cabinet tilt forward. "Quick, Vi!" I cried out. "The cabinet—it's going to fall!" Our arms lunged out, taking hold just in time to stop it from toppling over. But not before hearing a shard from the cracked glass door fall free and splinter onto the floor.

The sound of feet to stair ceased. An eerie stillness permeated the air. We held our breaths, awaiting his next move. After seconds that seemed an eternity, he suddenly bounded back down the steps. Having heard my voice call out to Vi, coupled with the sound of breaking glass, it would have been obvious to the man not only did someone lay in wait within but just who that someone was. Yours truly. What a debacle! We extricated ourselves from our confinement and headed downstairs, returning to our room in a disheartened mood.

"Well," said Vi, in trying to make the best of it, "at least he knows we're onto him. He'll have to be more careful now."

"I daresay we will as well."

"Think we might come to harm, do you?"

"There's always that possibility. But," I added in an

attempt to sound a note of reassurance, "don't forget, there's two of us and only one of him."

"Aye, you're right there," she said, managing a smile strictly for my benefit. It was obvious we were fooling no one but ourselves as to the danger we had put ourselves into.

I suppose we'd been up puttering about for no more than ten minutes or so the following morning before I noticed that a folded sheet of white paper had been slipped under our door.

" 'Ere, what's that you've got?" questioned Vi, as I bent down to retrieve it.

"Seems as though someone's left us a note sometime last night or early this morning," I answered as I unfolded the sheet. The paper itself told me nothing, other than it was Burbage House stationery left as a complimentary gesture in each room for the purposes of correspondence.

"A note? What's it say?"

I read the message and found myself quite stunned by its content. I then repeated it aloud for Vi. "It says," I announced, " 'Meet me tonight at midnight at the clock tower. I will answer all your questions.' It's signed," I added, " 'A friend.' "

"A friend, is it?" was her vitriolic response. "Oh, yes, we'll meet him at midnight—not ruddy likely! 'Ere," she said, "let's have a look at it. Why," she remarked on scanning the note, "it looks like it were written by a child. Printed all squiggly, it is."

"It's my guess," I replied, "that a right-handed person has used their left hand in the writing of it. No doubt as an added precaution against a check on their actual handwriting."

"Oh, he's clever, that one is," Vi was only too quick to state. "Though," she added, "I don't see how we could have checked the handwriting in any case."

"Mr. Burbage's registry book would have been one way," I answered. "But I take it you're of the opinion that it is our visitor from last night in the attic who penned it. And who now, in the sending of the note, seeks to lead us into some kind of trap.''

"Well, yes, 'course I do," she replied, seemingly taken aback that I should have even asked such a question. "Who else could it be?"

"Could it not have been written by a woman? It's impossible," I went on, with yet another glance at the note, "to determine the gender from this left-handed scrawl."

The idea that I thought it could have been written by a woman left my companion speechless. But only momentarily. "A woman! What woman? So help me, Em," she railed, "I don't know where you get these ideas of yours, I don't."

"Think about it, Vi," I urged. "If, as we suspect, one of the men lodged here has taken to roaming the attic at night, not to mention being responsible for the death of Mr. Latham when his presence was discovered by that gentleman, then his wife would surely be aware of her husband's absence during the midnight hours."

"Whose wife?"

"Would that I knew."

" 'Ere, let's see if I've got this straight," she said. "You're saying that if our Mr. X goes traipsing out of the room at night all dressed up like the captain, his wife would have to know what he's up to, right?"

"Exactly."

Violet turned the thought over in her mind for a moment or two before questioning me as to why the wife would want us to know what was going on. I told her I could only surmise that she, no doubt, sought our help in wanting to put a stop to it all before it led to yet another murder.

"Makes sense, I suppose," she admitted. "But," she said, "if it's like you say it is, it brings us back to whose wife she is. Mrs. Trefann, do you think?"

"Now hold on, Vi," I countered. "I didn't say it was written by a woman. Only that the possibility exists that it might have been. I could be dead wrong."

"*Dead* wrong? 'Ere," she said, "I don't like the sound of that."

I admitted with a smile it might have been a poor choice of words under the circumstances. "But I still can't help wondering," I added, "just what it is that our so-called ghost finds so interesting in the attic." Vi put forth the suggestion that he might be looking for some valuable artifact. Adding that she had read in the papers just the other day about some old biddy that had bought a supposedly worthless painting in one of the local flea markets, only to find out later it was actually a priceless Vermeer. While agreeing that such things do happen, I also made mention of the fact that I found it hard to believe that anything of value existed in the Burbage attic that would warrant taking a man's life. "But," I stated, "if it's answers we want, and we do, I suggest we take ourselves down to the tower tonight and have a chat with whoever it was that wrote the note. Are you game?"

"I suppose," she answered somewhat resignedly. "But whereabouts is this 'ere clock tower?"

"You remember," I reminded her, "we came upon it on our outing the other day. It sits in the middle of the square where the four roads meet."

"Oh, aye, that's right. Well, I don't suppose any harm could come to us there. Being out in the open as it is."

We kept pretty much to ourselves the rest of the day. Being mindful of our midnight meeting and the sleep we had lost the previous night, we took advantage of an afternoon nap to keep ourselves fit and fully awake for whatever it was that lay ahead. The only conversation we did engage in to any extent was with Mrs. Christie who, like we at the time, was descending the staircase on her way down to dinner. "Dining alone, are you, Mrs. Christie?" I asked as we continued down the steps.

"No, no," spoke the young woman. "My husband will be along shortly." She paused at the bottom and very cautiously turned her head in the direction of the kitchen door.

"You've heard then, I take it," I said. "About Mrs. Trefann's encounter with Sarah Hammond?"

" 'Deed I did," she replied. "Fair gives me goose bumps, it does, just thinking about it. Imagine, being face-to-face with a real live ghost! It's not something I'd want to do, I can tell you."

"A live ghost, you say?" chuckled my companion. "Don't know as how I'd rightly call her that."

"Well," she smiled, "you know what I mean."

" 'Course I do," answered Vi, returning the smile. "Why," she said, "this place is becoming a regular house of horrors, it is. Don't know why we don't all pack up and leave."

"Perhaps," added the woman, as we entered the dining area, "it might be best for all concerned if we did." As we had nothing further to say of any consequence to one another, we each proceeded to our assigned tables.

With supper at last over and done with, Vi and I headed back to our room to await our time of departure. At some time after eleven we set about getting ready. "Didn't think to bring along Doctor Watson's old army revolver, did you?" asked Violet as she peered into the dresser mirror to make a last-minute adjustment to her hat.

"No, Vi," I answered with a smile. "Somehow the thought of bringing a gun along with us on our holiday never occurred to me."

"Oh, aye, that's right!" she retorted. "Make a joke if you want. But you can't be too careful, that's what I say. And don't tell me," she carried on, "you're not nervous about all this 'meet me at midnight' business yourself."

"I'm apprehensive," I confessed. "But not to the point where I think we need to tote a firearm. Besides, as you say, what harm can come to us, being out in the open as it is?"

"Humph!" she snorted. "When did you start listening to me?"

"Come on, old girl," I laughed, "let's get a move on."

With all (apparently) in their rooms and bedded down

for the night, we left the house unnoticed and, being fortunate enough to find a cab after no more than a few minutes' wait, we climbed inside and headed off for our destination.

EIGHT

Hoofbeats and Horse Sense

➣ HAVING ARRIVED JUST before midnight we hastily took up our position at the base of the tower. As the minutes ticked by we found ourselves alone, irritable, and slightly damp from a northerly wind blowing, appropriately enough, up North Street, leaving smatterings of rain in its wake.

"Catch our death of cold, we will, standing out 'ere in the middle of the street," grumbled Vi. "What's the time now anyway, I wonder?" she added, pulling the collar of her coat up ever more around her.

"The time? Good heavens, Mrs. Warner," I responded in some annoyance, "this *is* a clock tower we're standing under."

"Oh, aye, right." She turned round and glanced upward, shielding her eyes from the drizzle as she did so, to announce the time as being thirteen minutes past twelve. "How long do you think we should wait?" she asked.

"Twelve-thirty at the latest," I snapped. "And not a minute longer." I then apologized to my companion for being a bit short with her. For, as I went on to explain, it

114

was not her I was annoyed with but the sender of the note.
To have us wait here at this hour of the night in weather
less than favorable was, in my opinion, simply intolerable.
It was then the thought occurred to me that perhaps the
note had been no more than a ruse to lead us away from
Burbage House. And if it had—for what purpose? That the
author of the note might rummage freely within the attic?
Or were there even more dire deeds being committed within
the house while we, having been played for the fool, stood
waiting in all innocence on a rain-swept street?

"Look," said Vi. "Down the road—seems like someone's coming this way."

"A woman, is it?" I asked.

"A man," she replied. " 'Least far as I can tell at this
distance."

At last, I thought. For, other than ourselves, he was the
only one on the street we had seen since our arrival. It had
to be him. Being a good block away, he continued toward
us at a slow, ambling pace which infuriated me even more.
On reaching a corner he turned unexpectedly (at least, unexpectedly to us) and headed down a side street. It was at
that point we saw the leash and the small dog that accompanied him. Within seconds both were lost to view.

"So much for that," stated Vi in a show of frustration.

"Here we stand," I announced, being as equally frus-
trated as she, "in the middle of the street, dripping wet,
and all we get for our trouble is seeing some poor old soul
out walking his dog." I glanced up at the clock to see that
the time now stood at twenty-seven minutes past midnight.
'I think," I added, "it's about time we called it a night."
Vi, need it be said, was of the same opinion.

"I just hope we can find ourselves a cab," she said.
'Don't fancy having to walk back."

"At least the rain seems to be easing up," I replied.

"Aye, but the wind's still got a bit of a nip to it."

"Speaking of cabs, we may just be in luck," I said, on
hearing the clatter of hoofbeats off in the distance. "Sounds
like he's coming up Queens Road. We might as well stay

here and flag him down as he drives by. Wait a minute,"
I said.

"I don't think that is a hansom. Sounds as if there's more
than one horse." As it came into view I could see that I'd
been right. It was a coach and four traveling, I would say,
at a goodly clip up the street. The driver, with hat pulled
low, coat collar turned up, and a scarf wrapped around the
bottom of his face, turned his head in our direction. He had
spotted us. Then again, how could he not, standing there
out in the open as we were.

With a sudden pull to the reins he swung the team of
horses in our direction and, with a cracking of his whip
over the backs of that thundering herd, proceeded to bear
down on us. As if in a hypnotic trance I stood there trans-
fixed as the galloping four with their windblown manes and
flaring nostrils continued to plunge ever forward. So close
were they now I swear I could feel their hot breath and
smell the sweat on those glistening hides.

"He's trying to kill us!" screamed Vi. She turned as if
to make a run for it. I grabbed her arm and drew her to
me. "Don't move," I managed to blurt out. "Not yet."
She looked at me as if I'd taken leave of my senses but
held her ground. I waited, trembling, until coach and horses
were almost upon us. "Now!" I cried out, pulling her back
and, as I did, sidestepping the both of us to safety. As the
coach raced past I could feel the hub of the wheels graze
my coat. It had been that close.

The two of us, though unhurt, were badly shaken, I can
tell you. We stood there holding and comforting each other
as the coach continued on in its mad dash down the street
before at last disappearing into the night.

"Tried to run us down, that's what he did!" Vi was
quick to state after we had regained a modicum of composure. I agreed, adding that it was apparent our captain
had now taken to the driving of horses through the streets
of Brighton as a means of eliminating the opposition. "You
think it was him then, do you?" she asked. "And not just
some lout who had a few too many?"

"Yes, I do; you saw the way he reined in the coach toward us. It was a deliberate attempt on his part to do away with us."

"Aye," she answered after a thoughtful pause, "I suppose you're right. Then the note we got, how do you explain—?"

"It was simply a way to get us down here," I announced, anticipating her question. "If he had been successful it would have appeared to the police that two women, crossing the street, had been struck down and killed by, as you yourself had first thought, a drunken driver. Fortunately for us his plan didn't succeed."

"Aye, thanks to you," she stated. "I was all for hightailing 'cross the street 'fore you stopped me."

"Yes, and just how far do you think you would have got trying to outrun four horses?" I asked. "If we had both taken off together we would have been quickly overtaken. Had we separated," I continued, "only one of us at best would be alive to tell the tale. "No," I added, "the only chance we had was to stand our ground until the last possible moment before sidestepping the onrush of horses. That way, he had no time at all to swing the coach in our direction."

"Aye, well, the long and short of it is we're still alive," she said. "That's the main thing."

I offered up the idea, though partly in jest, that when taking to our bed tonight we might pause and give a word or two of thanks to our guardian angels. Vi, in all seriousness, agreed wholeheartedly. Then again, why not? Lord knew, as perhaps did William and Albert, that we had escaped death or serious injury only by a wing and a prayer. Perhaps it had been more than just luck after all.

"And speaking of beds, as we were," said Vi, "what wouldn't I give to be all snuggled down and cozy-like right about now."

"As would I," I added. "Though when we will be, I haven't the slightest. At this hour we may have quite a walk ahead of us." But in due course a hansom did come clip-clopping its way down the street and grateful we were for the ride back.

"It's getting on to teatime," announced my companion on the following afternoon. "Coming downstairs then, are you?"

"No," I answered, "you go ahead if you like. But be a luv, would you, and bring a tea up for me on your way back?"

"Why, what are you going to do?"

"I thought I'd stay here in our room and set down the events as they unfolded since we've been here. Make notes, that type of thing. As far as I'm concerned," I stated most vehemently, setting myself down at the small writing desk and placing stationery, ink bottle, and pen out before me, "this wretched business has gone on long enough. Besides," I added, "I do not take kindly to either one of us being the target for murder."

"Well," said Vi, "if you can make heads or tails of it all, good luck to you, is all I can say. See you later then, luv."

"And don't forget my tea," I called out as she exited the room.

So there I sat, going over in my mind and setting down on paper what had happened, when it happened, and who said what about this and who said what about that, while trying to find some common thread to it all. Something was hidden in the attic and someone was going to an awful lot of trouble to find it. Even murder. And, as in our case, attempted murder as well. But what was hidden, who had hidden it, and who was it that searched for it? The only possible explanation I could come up with as to what treasure lay upstairs was the diamond ring known as the Star of Hyderabad. But, as I told myself, the theft of the ring occurred a good many years ago. Why search for it now? Besides, according to the inspector, the ring had been passed along to an accomplice who, by all accounts, would have sold it to a dealer in stolen gems. He, in turn, would have cut it down into smaller stones in order to place it back on the market. So much for that idea.

With a sigh, I once again went over the events as they had taken place with a feeling of utter helplessness in knowing I was no nearer to understanding the mystery of it all than I had been since Vi had left a good half hour ago. As I began to delve deeper into it a thought suddenly occurred to me. "Of course!" I exclaimed aloud to an empty room. "That has to be it!" Although I hadn't at that point sorted it all out in any chronological order I felt— no, I *knew*—I was on the right track. At that moment in walked Vi. Empty-handed, I might add.

"Oh, no," she wailed in the realization of her gaffe. "I forgot your tea. That's me all over, that is." She turned round to leave. "Be back in a minute," she said.

"No, no, forget about the tea," I sang out, scarcely able to control my excitement at what I now believed had happened. "I can always get it later."

Violet eased herself down on the side of the bed while continuing to eye me somewhat warily. "I didn't expect you to be all smiles and chuckles," she said at last. "Thought you'd have summat to say 'bout me not bringing you up your tea. You can be sharp sometimes, you can, Emma Hudson."

"The tea's not important," I was quick to assure her. "What *is* is that I believe I may have part of the answer as to what's been going on around here."

My companion brightened up considerably on hearing the news. "Know who it is who's pretending to be the ghost of the captain, do you?" she asked.

"Well, no," I hedged. "At least not yet."

"Oh."

Her singular response had the effect of quickly deflating me. "But," I responded, trying to regain a degree of my former enthusiasm, "I think I may have put together a large chunk of the puzzle."

"Oh, aye? Well, I suppose that's summat at least, isn't it, luv?" she replied, managing a faint smile.

While I found her reply a trifle condescending, I could well understand her dwindling lack of interest. For Vi, as well I knew, the one overriding goal was to reveal the identity of the man masquerading as the late Captain John Hammond. But, as I explained to her, we needed an overall picture of the events that had taken place up to this time before certain segments of the puzzle, including who our mystery ghost was, became clear to us. "Would you not agree?" I asked. She nodded, albeit somewhat halfheartedly. "Now then," I said, "let's start at the beginning, shall we?"

"You mean with us signing into Burbage's here?"

"A little further back than that, I'm afraid," I replied. "The beginning I speak of goes back to the night the Star of Hyderabad was stolen from the Windermere estate." And in the saying of it, I knew full well the response I'd receive. I was not disappointed.

" 'Ere, what's this you're saying?" she sang out. "Why, that were a good ten years ago! What's all that got to do with us being nearly run over last night? Or anything else for that matter, eh?"

"If you let me get on with it," I answered in manner calm, "I'll be happy to explain." Save for a mumble or two, she said no more.

"From what the inspector has told us," I began, "we have a thief, Charlie Allbright by name, who, working in collusion with the upstairs maid at the estate, steals the Hyderabad ring that had been left unattended on her ladyship's dresser. He then takes off to Burbage's to await the arrival in two days' time of the maid, Annie Potter."

"Until things cool down like," spoke Vi.

"Exactly."

"But why Burbage's?" she asked.

I answered that I couldn't see any significance in the fact that he had chosen to stay here. It might just as well have been any one of the number of lodging houses, bed and breakfast inns, or hotels within the area. "But whatever the reason," I added, "Burbage's it was. Meanwhile, unbeknownst to Allbright, the maid has confessed her part in it and reveals to the police where her paramour is staying.''

"But," continued Vi, now showing more of an interest in the tale, "he's tipped off by his pal that the inspector is on his way over. That's when this 'ere Allbright hands the ring over to this other bloke so's he wouldn't be caught with it in his possession. Right?''

"Wrong!" I stated most forcefully.

" 'Ere," she shot back, "what do you mean, wrong? According to the inspector, that's the way it happened.''

"And that," I announced, "is where the inspector and I part company. The story of there being another man," I went on, "as the inspector himself has stated, is simply what he believes must have happened. It was this second-man theory of his," I informed her, "that kept sending me up a blind alley. But if we discount the idea of another man being involved in the theft then everything falls into place.''

"How d'you mean?''

"The longer Allbright waits for Annie here at Burbage House," I explained, "the more nervous he becomes. And why not? He has in his possession one of the world's most fabulous gems. Should anything go wrong with his plan and it's found on his person or in his room the game would be up. So he hides it where it won't be found. Intending to retrieve it later when he and Annie take off for London.''

"So," said Vi, continuing on with the story, "when the police show up, having been tipped off by the maid where he is, they don't find this 'ere Star of whatever it is, on him or in his room.''

"True. But," I stated, "they *do* find the brooch he nicked that same night from her ladyship's bedroom. That, in itself, was enough to earn him his prison sentence. As I say," I continued, "once I had tossed aside the idea of Allbright and another man working in tandem, it all seemed to fall into place. There was no other man.''

" 'Ere," she asked, "how'd you figure all this out any-way?''

"Good old-fashioned horse sense," I stated. "If you'll

forgive the expression," I added somewhat sardonically, alluding to our harrowing encounter the previous night with coach and four.

Vi screwed her face up in thought while mentally reviewing all she had heard. " 'Ere, wait a minute," she said at last. "If what you say is true, then this 'ere Allbright bloke must have hid the diamond ring—in the attic?"

"That's my guess," I replied. "And I believe it's the right one. For what else could he have done with it? It would have been the only possible place for him to hide it."

"Aye, but there's summat wrong 'ere," she said. "It can't be him who's looking for it now. He'd know where he put it. 'Sides that, from what the inspector told us, he died in prison. Unless you think it's his ghost that's—"

"Hardly. I think we have enough spirits to contend with without adding another one to the list. Besides, of what use would a diamond be to a ghost?"

"Aye, makes sense when you put it that way. So," she said, "where do we go from 'ere?"

"To Charlie Allbright's prison cell."

"Eh?"

"Figuratively, Vi, not literally," I added with a smile. "Now then, let's go back in time, shall we? There sits Allbright in his cell year after year," I began, "confident in the knowledge that when he's released from prison the gem will be waiting for him right where he left it. He tells no one of its existence."

"What about his cell mate?" asked Vi. "Eddie something or other."

"Dobbs," I answered. "Eddie Dobbs."

"Aye. Think Allbright might have told him, do you? Being his cell mate and all?"

"Good heavens, Violet," I replied, "that would have been the last person he'd tell. Suppose Dobbs escaped from prison or was released before Allbright—he'd be in a position to retrieve the gem for himself, thank you very much. No," I went on, "Allbright would have kept his secret.

Though I daresay Dobbs knew about the actual theft itself, as would have the other inmates."

"But they'd think, like the inspector, the diamond had been cut up and sold. Is that what you're saying?"

"Precisely. Although, as his cell mate over the years, Dobbs must have had his own suspicions as to whether the gem still existed or not. Be that as it may," I continued, "Charlie Allbright never does live to walk out of prison a free man to claim his prize. His prison cot is now his death-bed. As he lays dying from the onset of a heart attack he manages to gasp out to his mate where the gem is hidden. The constable himself," I added, "made mention of hearing Allbright mumble a word or two to Dobbs before he expired, as you may remember him telling us."

"Aye, that's right," she confirmed. "Haddock, he said. But like I said at the time, people say all sorts of queer things when they're dying. Rambling, they calls it."

"Oh, Vi," I groaned, "I thought it would be fairly obvious what he was saying. Not *haddock* but *attic*. He was telling him the diamond lay within the attic. As I say," I went on, "Dobbs would have known about the robbery at the Windermere estate and the fact that Allbright had been picked up at Burbage's without the ring in his possession. Now here was the man gasping out the word *attic*. It wouldn't have taken much for his old cell mate to put two and two together. But *where* in the attic? Unfortunately for Dobbs, Allbright died before he could find out. However," I added, "he could at least take comfort in the fact that he now knew the site if not the actual spot where it lay hidden."

"Fat lot of good it did him," announced Vi. "Wasn't he the one the sergeant said was murdered in some pub just a few weeks ago after getting out of prison?"

"The very same," I answered.

"Well," she said, "there you are then. We've come to a dead end, we have."

"Not necessarily," I replied, pausing only to fill a glass from the pitcher of water that had been sitting on the dresser since early that morning. How I wished Vi had remembered the tea.

"I could still pop downstairs and bring us both back a cuppa, if you like," she offered, as if reading my mind.

"No, no," I answered, managing a brave smile as I gulped down the lukewarm liquid, "this is fine." Besides, I had no intention of calling an intermission for tea while being caught up in my analysis of the situation.

"Well, go on then," said Vi. "You were saying—?"

"That we're not necessarily at a dead end. At least, not quite. Dobbs, as we know," I continued, "was last seen drinking with another man in some pub or other before his body was found in back of it with his head bashed in. It's this other man we're looking for," I stated. "The one last seen with him."

"We are?" she asked in all innocence. "Why?"

"Because, my dear Mrs. Warner," I informed her in grand fashion, "that man is our Captain Hammond!"

My announcement had the effect on her of total surprise combined, I might add, with an equal amount of skepticism. " 'Ere," she said, "just how do you figure that?"

"Think about it," I replied. I reached for the water glass again, thought better of it, set it down, and continued on. "Dobbs, on getting out of prison, now knows where the legendary Star of Hyderabad resides. In the attic of Burbage House. But the question remains, how to get it? He can't go waltzing in as bold as you please and start rummaging about upstairs. He needs a plan. Remember," I added, "Eddie Dobbs was a confidence man. A schemer of schemes. But he's just come out of prison. How is he to register at Burbage's with no money to speak of and possessing, I daresay, naught but the clothes on his back? Our Mr. Dobbs needs a confederate. Perhaps the man he was seen drinking with was someone he knew, perhaps an ex-convict. In any event," I went on, "Dobbs must have let him in on the secret of the hidden gem. It's my belief that it was Dobbs's idea to have this other man register at Burbage's as a guest. If he's married, I daresay he'd bring his wife along simply for appearance's sake. If not, a lady friend would do just as well."

"Oh," said Vi, stepping in, "I shouldn't think so. Mrs. Burbage isn't the kind to allow anyone who's not man and wife to—"

"Oh, Vi," was my exasperated response, "she wouldn't be any the wiser, would she? It doesn't take much to sign in as Mr. and Mrs., now does it?"

"Well," she sniffed, "I don't know as how I like the sound of all this."

"Nevertheless," I carried on, "the plan would be that once they're settled in, the 'husband,' if you will, would be free to search the upstairs attic. Now whether the idea of dressing up like the ghost of Captain Hammond was his idea or that of Dobbs, I haven't the foggiest, though my bet is that it was Dobbs. But it did, and still does, for that matter, work to the man's advantage. Noises heard up in the attic, you say? Must be the old captain roaming about. Quite a brilliant idea really, when you think about it."

"Aye," nodded Vi, "it all seems to make sense the way you explain it."

"Why, thank you, Violet." I beamed.

" 'Cept for one or two things," she added.

Oh, dear, shot down again. "And what would that be?" I asked with a resigned sigh.

"Why," she questioned, "did this 'ere other man you're talking about kill Dobbs? If, as you say, they were all in it together?"

"Oh," I said, brightening up, "that's easy enough to explain. Once he knew everything Dobbs knew, what need had he for a partner? With Dobbs out of the way, he and his lady friend—and she may very well be his wife for all we know—sign themselves into Burbage's and the hunt begins. There's no need to divide with Dobbs the monies gained from the selling of the gem once it's been found. And the other?"

"Eh?"

"You said there was one or two other things."

"Oh, just that this 'ere mystery man of yours," she said, "would have to be from Brighton, wouldn't he? I mean," she added, "if Dobbs knew him and everything, it seems to me—"

"Yes, I agree," I replied. "I imagine he would be one of the locals from around here."

"Aye, but the thing is," she continued, "everyone who's signed in at Burbage's is down here from London."

She was right. Everything hinged on him being a local resident of Brighton. I was left completely stunned. I had no answer for her. Fortunately, the absence of a response on my part lasted only momentarily. "Ah, but my dear Violet," I airily responded, as if the question barely warranted an answer, "it's a simple matter for anyone to sign in as being from London. We ourselves could have written in Timbuktu as our residence and who would have been the wiser?"

"Mrs. Burbage, for one," she said.

I made a face. "You know what I mean," I replied.

"Aye," she smiled. "Someone's registered as being from London when he's right 'ere from Brighton. But who?"

"Who indeed?" I replied. "That's the question, isn't it? As for now," I added, on rising to a standing position, "I think it's time we headed off for tea."

"Tea?" she questioned, easing herself off the edge of the bed. "It's getting on to suppertime."

"All the better. In any event, we'll continue our little discussion when we get back. Mind, not a word of what we've been talking about during mealtime."

"Even the walls have ears, is that what you're saying?"

"Yes," I replied. "And unfortunately, so does everyone else."

NINE

Step by Step

⟨҈⟩ OUR SUPPER THAT evening consisted of rabbit and red currant jelly. And while I found, as did Vi, the sauce to be somewhat thin, that is not to say that we did not enjoy every last morsel, as did our fellow guests who set about devouring their meal with great gusto. For all were present within the dining room, save one. Mrs. Christie. Her husband, poor man, was left to dine alone in silence with scarcely an upward glance beyond the perimeters of his table.

As we sat back, relaxing and enjoying our tea after having finished our meal, Mrs. Burbage entered the room bearing a tray of scrumptious gooseberry fool desserts. Two of which she set down before us.

"Oh, lovely," gushed Vi.

I took the opportunity of the woman's presence to inquire as to the reason for Mrs. Christie's absence. Discreetly, mind, for the husband sat no more than a table away.

"She's taken herself back to London," I was quietly informed after some hesitancy on her part. "On an urgent family matter, he said." It was clear that the woman felt uncomfortable passing along information behind the back, as it were, of one guest to another. "Enjoy your dessert," she added as a parting remark.

I was not about to let her get away so quickly. "You never spoke to Mrs. Christie herself, then?" I asked.

"Never saw her," she answered. "Nor did Mr. Burbage. I take it that it was all pretty quick-like. Things like that happen. Now, if you'll excuse me—"

I continued to press on. "So you've no idea what this urgent family matter is then?"

"No, I do not, Mrs. Hudson," she replied somewhat testily. "Nor did I ask. That would be prying, wouldn't it?"

I took her meaning and said no more, other than to offer up a word of hope that the urgent family matter would prove to be nothing too serious. With that, she was off to another table, leaving the two of us to delve deep into our dessert.

"It's easy enough to see what happened, isn't it?" spoke Vi, after giving one last lick to her spoon. "The Christies had some sort of a row and she up and left him. And who could blame either one of them, eh? Why," she said, "with what's been going on around 'ere it's enough to set anybody's nerves on edge."

"And that," I added, "is just one more reason to clear up this whole ghastly business once and for all. Now, the way I see it—"

" 'Ere," she said, cutting in, "I thought we weren't going to talk about you know what, 'til we got back to our room."

"And quite right you are, Violet," I replied. "Come along then if you're finished. Let's see if we can make some sense of it all upstairs."

Once back in our room Vi returned to her perch on the side of the bed and I, after removing a pillow from the bed and setting it on one of the two stiff-backed chairs, took my place at the small writing desk. "Now, what I believe we should concentrate on," I said, riffling through my notes, "is who would be the most logical person within the house to be masquerading as the ghost of Captain Hammond. For by unmasking the ghost,'' I added, ''we unmask the murderer as well.'' Vi agreed but confessed that she wouldn't know where to begin. I put forth the suggestion that we start with Mr. Burbage.

''What?'' she exclaimed. ''Why, you must be joking. Big lummock like him? I can tell you right off, I can, it weren't him I seen walking the hall that night.''

''From the description you gave of him at the time,'' I replied, ''I daresay he wasn't.''

''Well then?''

''Have you ever given thought to the idea,'' I asked, ''that Burbage might have someone secretly in his employ—someone he lets in at night? It could be this other man, in the guise of the old sea captain, that you saw.''

Vi pondered the thought. ''Then if that's the case,'' she said, ''it has to be Burbage who was seen drinking with Dobbs in the pub. And when he learns from him about the hidden diamond in his attic, he kills him and hires this other bloke to snoop around for it. Is that what you're saying?''

''What I'm saying,'' I informed her, ''is that it *could* be our Mr. Burbage. Remember, what we are doing here is merely theorizing. Though it would be safe to assume, if it is Burbage,'' I added, ''he would never reveal to this second man the true value of the gem. Another point to take into account,'' I continued, ''is the description of the man seen drinking with Dobbs on that fatal day. I believe he was described by one of the eyewitnesses as being a man somewhat rotund in appearance, as is Mr. Burbage himself.''

''Aye,'' she replied. ''But, if you remember, the inspector also told us there were those at the pub who said he was thin, short, tall—''

''Yes, yes, I know what you're saying,'' I interjected. ''And I have to admit it's the weakest link that chains him to the crime. But,'' I added, ''consider this from Dobbs's point of view: what better man could he have singled out for his plan of retrieving the diamond than the owner of

Burbage House himself? And," I continued on, "if we stick to our theory that the murderer is from Brighton, Samuel Burbage and his wife are the only ones we know for sure that reside here. Our host would be well aware of who he could hire to seek out the missing gem."

"True enough, I suppose," answered Violet after a moment or two of mulling it over. "But as for it being Burbage—" She shook her head. "I just can't see it," she said.

"Mind now," I was quick to state, "I'm not saying it *is* him. It's just that we have to look at each of our suspects on an individual basis. Do you recall," I asked, "the reaction we received from both Mr. Burbage and his wife when we informed them of your seeing what you believed at the time was a ghostly figure walking the hall?"

"Aye," she said. "Tried to fluff it off, they did."

"Exactly. Simply the spirit of a certain Captain Hammond it was, they said. A harmless soul who, according to them, would pose neither to us or our fellow guests a threat to either life or limb. The idea being not to have any of their fainthearted guests panic on seeing him nor to have their more stouthearted guests seek him out within the attic."

"So, if anyone hears noises upstairs," added Vi, "they'd believe it's the captain wandering about and think no more of it."

"That would be my guess. And if we continue on with the theory that the Burbages are behind it all," I stated, "they made the mistake of not taking Mr. Latham into account."

"Mr. Latham?" questioned Vi. "How d'you mean?"

"From what that gentleman told me before his untimely death," I replied, "he was of the opinion that it was not Captain Hammond who had suddenly taken to haunting the attic. On that fatal night, as we now know, he decided to investigate for himself the sounds heard from above. Arriving upstairs, he encounters the man disguised as the captain. Our murderer knows that if Latham leaves the attic alive the game is up. A fight ensues and, well, you know the rest.''

"Aye, only too well,'' confirmed Violet. "And here's a thought for you,'' she added. "Remember us stepping out into the hall on the night Mr. Latham was murdered?''

"You mean when we were on our way up to investigate the sound I believed was that of a body falling to the floor?''

"Which it was,'' she said. "And who did we meet in the hallway?''

"Mr. Burbage,'' I answered. "Who informed us he was on his way up to check out the noise as well.''

"Aye, but was he?''

"Then it's your thought,'' I replied, "that he wasn't on his way upstairs but that he simply stepped out into the hall on hearing our voices to question what it was we were up to.''

"After,'' she was quick to state, "hiding the bloke who killed Latham in his room.''

"If I read you right,'' I said, "you're saying the murderer descended the attic stairs and made his way to the Burbages' room where he and his wife whisked him safely inside. By the time we came out into the hall,'' I carried on, "Mr. Jones was already up in the attic after having taken it upon himself to do a little investigating on his own.''

"And when we arrive in the attic along with Burbage,'' continued Vi, "we see Mr. Jones bending over the body of Mr. Latham. But Burbage, knowing Jones is as innocent as we, starts in accusing him of murder.''

"Good thinking, Vi,'' was my congratulatory response. "That could very well be what happened.''

"Aye, well,'' she beamed, "the old girl does come up with an idea or two once in a while, you know. One thing though,'' she questioned. "What about this 'ere bloke that tried to run us down?'' My reply was to state that by all accounts he would have been none other than the man Burbage hired to seek out the diamond. "So,'' said she, readjusting herself to a more comfortable position on our less than comfortable bed, "it's the Burbages then, is it?"

"It could very well be," I replied. "Then again—" I shrugged as an indication of it still being all up in the air. "Remember, Violet," I said, "at this point we're simply taking it step by step. Don't forget," I added, "there are others as well who also fill the bill as being our less than supernatural ghost."

"Like who?" she asked.

"Pick a name," I said.

"Mr. Jones," she replied.

"All right then, let's see what we have on young Mr. Jones. According to him," I said, glancing over my notes to reacquaint myself with what I had previously written, "he's originally from Wales. He left there for London where he subsequently found employment as a printer's assistant. He's recently married. His wife's name being—" I flipped over the page. "Cathie."

"From what you were telling me after having your little chat with him," spoke Vi, "it's this new wife of his that's left him to cool his heels here in Brighton while she sulks back in London over some lovers' quarrel they had. Right?"

"Yes, that's true," I replied. "And I do hope they get back together, here or in London, for that matter. He did say," I added, setting my notes aside, "that he'd written her in the hope that they could at least have a few days here."

"What with his and Mr. Christie's marital problems, I'd say our male lodgers aren't having all that much luck with their women," announced Violet.

"Yes, I'd have to agree with you there," I answered with a smile, adding that Burbage House was not exactly the place I'd recommend to anyone as a honeymoon haven.

"Shame though, really," she said. "Our Mr. Jones seems like a nice enough young chap. Who's next, then?"

Who's next, then? Is that what she said? "My dear Mrs.

Warner," I announced, "we've yet to begin. Let's dig a little deeper into his story, shall we?"

" 'Ere now!" she sputtered in a show of indignation. "You don't think Mr. Jones has got anything to do with what's been going on around 'ere, do you? You're wrong there, if that's what you think."

"What I think," I informed her, "is neither here nor there. Mr. Jones, as is the case with everyone else residing here, remains under a cloud of suspicion just as long as the murderer continues to stalk the halls. Why," I continued, "it was you yourself who offered up his name as a suspect no more than a minute ago."

"Well, not so much as a suspect like," she admitted. "He were just someone I thought we could pass over quickly."

"Pass over quickly? And why is that? Because," I said, in answer to my own question, "you believe he's a nice young chap. Is that it?"

"He *is* Welsh," she stated in defense of her position. "And you said yourself, Emma Hudson, the one we're looking for would be from around these 'ere parts. And," she added in that snippy way of hers, "the last time I looked at a map, Wales wasn't all that close to Brighton."

"He's *originally* from Wales," I reminded her. "He may very well have left there and settled down, not in London as he told us, but here in Brighton itself."

"But," she countered, "he's got himself a wife in London, he has."

"Oh, Violet," I sighed, "he might just as well have said he has a wife in Timbuktu. And how would we be any the wiser?"

"You and your Timbuktu," she stated. "That's the second time you mentioned it. Whereabouts is it, anyway?"

"I haven't the foggiest," I confessed. "Africa—I think. But," I added in some annoyance, "that's hardly the point, is it? Let's concentrate on Mr. Jones. This time around," I said, "Peter Jones is the guilty party, not Mr. Burbage."

"Let's hear it then," was my companion's less than enthusiastic response.

"Right. Now then," I began, "Dobbs gets out of prison and looks up his old drinking mate, Jones. Over a brew or two, Dobbs tells Jones about the Star of Hyderabad he believes is hidden somewhere within the attic of Burbage House. And of his plan of needing someone to check in to find it. When he's finished with his tale, it occurs to Jones that if Dobbs were out of the way—"

"If he was murdered, you mean," she interjected.

"Yes, all right, murdered then," I replied. "He, Jones, would be the sole possessor of the diamond."

"Think Mr. Jones would murder a man for a ring, do you?" she asked in a way that made it clear she was obviously of a different opinion.

"Good heavens, Violet," I snapped back. "There are people on the streets of London every day who are murdered for less than a pound note. This Star of Hyderabad is worth millions!" She had no ready response so I pressed on. "Jones bashes Dobbs's head in at the back of the pub. Then, with that gruesome business out of the way, he signs himself into Burbage's using a London address. And," I added, "so that it would not appear odd that he should be vacationing here in Brighton for a fortnight by himself, he tells the story of a wife in London who may, or may not, be joining him at a later date."

"A wife who doesn't exist—is that what you're saying?"

"Yes," I answered. "If indeed he really is our ghostly captain."

"If he is," questioned Vi, "why did he write his wife a letter asking her to come down, if there is no wife?"

"But did he write a letter? We've only his word for that," I replied. "If he did he would have left it at the desk with Mr. Burbage to see that it got mailed."

"We'd best check with Burbage then," she advised. "Just to see if he did." I agreed. "So," continued Vi, "to go along with your story of Jones murdering Dobbs, he must have also—?"

"Been responsible for the death of Mr. Latham? If that's what you're asking, the answer's yes. Mr. Latham," I went on, "arrives up in the attic and discovers Jones in the garb of the captain. A fight breaks out between the two men and Latham falls, striking his head on the iron leg of the sewing machine table, the impact of it killing him. From our room we hear the noise of his body falling and, on our way up to check it out, run into Mr. Burbage in the hall. Meanwhile, Jones has discarded the seafaring coat and hat he's been wearing, stuffing them, no doubt, into the nearest trunk. When we and Mr. Burbage arrive on the scene," I added, "we see Jones bending over the body, proclaiming his innocence to one and all."

"Aye, that's right," announced Vi. "According to him, Mr. Latham must have seen the ghost, got frightened-like, and, stumbling back, fell, striking his head."

"Which of course," I stated, "is pure nonsense."

"It is? 'Ere, what makes you say that?"

"For the simple reason," I explained, "that Mr. Latham had seen the ghost many a time over the years as a sad, pathetic spirit who appeared in life form to him on a number of occasions. Why then," I asked, "would he suddenly become frightened to the extent of falling down from a heart attack when confronting him in the attic? It doesn't make sense."

"I suppose it doesn't," she grudgingly admitted.

"And the annoying part of it all," I continued, "is that we would have known once and for all who our ghost was if only we hadn't inadvertently made our presence known on the night we hid ourselves up in the attic."

"And what with him knowing it's us up there," added Vi, continuing on with my thought, "he slips a note under our door saying where to meet him. Then hires himself a coach and tries to run us down. But," she questioned, "if all this is true, that makes him as guilty as Burbage. But it can't be the both of them. Which one is it then?"

"Perhaps neither," I answered. "Remember, there are others to consider as well. Let's put the Christies under the magnifying glass, so to speak, shall we?"

"From what I remember them telling us," said Vi, "they're the owners of a small fish and chip shop. Forget where—back in London someplace. At least," she chuckled, "we know it's not the same Christies who own the shop we popped into the other day."

"That's something at least," I agreed. "Though it doesn't necessarily mean that they themselves are not from Brighton." I picked up my notes and ran a finger down the page. "Ah, here it is," I said. "Fish and chips—Mews Lane—Strand."

"Aye, that's right," confirmed Vi. "Mews Lane. A street running off the Strand, they said."

"Never heard of it," I said. "You?"

"Mews Lane? Not right offhand," she answered. "But it sounds like it could be right. Give 'em the benefit of the doubt, I say."

"You're more generous than I," I announced.

"How so?"

"My dear Mrs. Warner," I informed her, "if we are to carry out a proper investigation we can hardly accept what we hear from those under suspicion of committing a crime to be true."

"You've got a suspicious nature, you have, Emma Hudson," my companion was quick to state. "And no mistake."

A suspicious nature? I didn't know if I quite liked the sound of that. "Perhaps *inquisitive* might be the better word," I replied.

"Have it your own way," she said. "All I know is that Mews Lane has the ring of truth about it."

"There's one way of finding out," I stated. "And that's to get hold of a London street map. I'd best jot that down," I added, penciling in a reminder to myself. "So's I won't forget."

"So, you're saying Mr. Christie's our murderer now, right?" asked Vi as I set my sheet aside.

"For all intents and purposes, yes," I replied. "We now have Christie murdering Dobbs for the same reason as had Burbage and Jones. With the exception that he signs in here with the woman we know as Mrs. Christie. Who she might very well be."

"Just an innocent couple down here on a holiday from London to enjoy the sea air, is that it?"

"Innocent?" I quizzed. "That's the question, isn't it? One thing I find strange was their not putting in an appearance on the night the police arrived to investigate the cause of Mr. Latham's death. But it might make sense," I added, "if we go along with our theory that they are the guilty party. It's Christie now who, in the garb of the captain, is indirectly the cause of Mr. Latham's death."

"Well, whether it's him or not," spoke Vi, "he couldn't be considered a real murderer like, could he? I mean," she went on to explain, "Mr. Latham died when falling back and striking his head."

"The man fell back," I reminded her, "after being struck by our so-called ghost. That in itself makes him an accessory to murder. And," I continued, "if it's a charge of murder you're after, don't forget a very dead Eddie Dobbs. One could hardly call being struck down from behind with a rock an accidental death. We also have," I added, harking back to our near-death encounter with four wild-eyed horses, "a charge of attempted murder waiting in the wings for him."

I then continued on with my theory by having Christie racing back down the attic stairs to the sanctity of his room. "As to the reason for him and his wife not putting in an appearance, why would they?" I asked of Vi. "The last thing they'd want to do," I answered for her, "is to be interrogated. A wrong word might prove to be their undoing. And for all we know, they might also have a criminal record and be known to the police."

"Never thought of that," she admitted. "But just what

was the reason they gave us the next day for not having shown up? I've forgotten."

I returned to my notes. "According to the Christies," I answered, "he had seen the spirit of John Hammond in the hall earlier that night. The sight of which had upset him to the point where, on hearing further commotions out in the hall later on that same night, they thought it best to simply remain put."

"Makes sense," commented Vi, nodding her head in agreement with the explanation.

"Does it? I wonder?"

"What makes you say that?"

"Listen to what Mr. Christie had to say when coming upon the captain," I answered on once more returning to my notes. " 'Captain's eyes burned into mine—wicked sneer on his face. Raised his arm,' " I read on, " 'and ascended upwards toward the ceiling—disappeared.' What rot! Quite a remarkable feat, wouldn't you say, for a ghost who, in reality, is as mortal as we. According to Mr. Latham," I continued, "whose opinion I respected and who lived in this house for a good many years, Captain Hammond was but a lost soul who, up until a few years back, would appear for a few seconds, at best, at the top of the landing. But," I carried on, "from what Mr. Christie would have us believe, the old captain is now some demonic spectre from the netherworld complete with evil sneer and coal-burning eyes. Really, I ask you."

"But," questioned Vi, "whyever would Mr. Christie make up such a story?"

"Unlike Mr. Burbage," I explained, "who, if guilty, would have us believe that the Hammonds, or in particular, the captain, is harmless and we should let him go about his business, Mr. Christie, on the other hand, takes the opposite tack. Albeit for the same reason. Be frightened of him, he tells us. Don't go near him. In other words, do not attempt to follow him."

"Aye, I see," she said. "If anyone hears him upstairs they'd best throw the covers over their head and let him be. That way," she added, "he can hunt out the diamond without anyone popping in on him unexpected-like."

"Yes, exactly. But, of course," I reminded her, "there are two sides to every coin."

"Which means?"

"Let's say he's innocent," I replied. "He comes out of his room, sees the man he believes is the ghost of Captain Hammond, and rushes back inside. The fanciful tale he tells," I explained, "is, in fact, nothing more than an attempt on his part to gain a little attention for himself. The more impressive the story, the more impressive the story-teller."

"But," said Vi, "if he *is* our ghost, it's him what drove the horses and left the note under our door."

"Him or his wife," I added.

"What? Drove the horses?"

"Oh, Vi, for heaven's sake. No, left the note."

"Oh. Right. And speaking of Mrs. Christie," she carried on, "what's happened to her then, eh? I mean, disappearing the way she did. Think it was a row they had, do you?" she asked. "Or could it be summat to do with this 'ere Star of Eiderdown?"

"Hyderabad," I corrected her. "As to why she suddenly took herself from the scene," I answered, "I've no idea. It's a puzzle, all right." I then suggested we turn our thoughts aside from the Christies to concentrate on the Trefanns.

" 'Fore we start," spoke Vi, "I've got to see about getting meself a little more comfortable." She took herself off the side of the bed and, on removing her pillow, propped it up against the back of the remaining chair. "Ah, that's better," she said, easing herself down on the seat with a satisfied smile. "Me back was killing me."

While I expressed sympathy, I also made mention of the fact, to which she agreed, that while it would have been best for comfort's sake had we taken ourselves down to the leather-bound chairs of the reading room, the privacy we sought could very well be jeopardized. The topic then turned to the Trefanns.

"He's a postman, right?" was Violet's opening remark.

"So he says," I replied. "And I've no reason to doubt that he isn't. At least, not yet," I added. "But where? In Brighton? Or in London, as he claims?"

"Still think our murderer is from around these parts, do you?"

I responded by questioning how he could not be. "Think about it, Vi," I said. "If Dobbs were to take someone into his confidence with respect to his plan for retrieving the diamond, I find it extremely doubtful he would approach a tourist who arrived but a week or so ago. He would have had to have known the man previous to his confinement in prison. As for Mr. Trefann," I continued, "he may or may not have had a prison record as well. But even if he hadn't, I daresay he could have been easily swayed by the thought of becoming a very wealthy man."

"Aye," she agreed. "Doubt if it would have taken much persuasion on Dobbs's part when you figures what a postman's wages are."

"My thoughts exactly," I readily agreed.

"Still," she hedged, "I dunno. "Trefann as the murderer? He's not all that big a man, is he?"

"It's true," I replied, "that he hasn't the height or weight of, say, Mr. Jones, for example. But how big a man do you have to be to pick up a rock and strike another on the back of the head with it? Remember this as well," I added, "it wasn't a clenched fist that ultimately killed Mr. Latham but a wrought-iron leg."

Vi wagged a knowing finger in my direction. "I think," she said, "you're honing in on Mr. Trefann as being the one behind it all."

"Not at all," I was quick to state. "I'm only saying the possibilities are there."

"Though when you think of it," spoke Vi, "he is a bit of a quiet bloke, isn't he? 'Course, I suppose that's neither here nor there. But it's always the quiet ones that make me nervous like.''

I reminded my companion that, withdrawn though he might have been, he didn't hesitate to announce to one and all on the night we discovered Mr. Latham's body that he too had seen the ghost of Captain Hammond.

''Aye, that's right,'' replied Vi, nodding her head in the remembrance of it. ''I'd forgotten 'bout that. 'Least,'' she said, ''he didn't give us some song and dance about the captain flying up to the ceiling, as Mr. Christie did.''

My reply was that Trefann didn't really need to expound on his story. I put it to her that the mere fact of his mentioning to us of having seen the ghostly form of the captain, while we and the others stood huddled in horror round Mr. Latham's corpse, had the desired effect he sought.

''So, what you're saying,'' spoke Vi, ''is that the others will associate death with the captain and be mindful of him.''

''Yes, something like that,'' I answered.

''The thing of it is, when it comes to who did what to who, I'm too trustful,'' announced Violet.

''Trustful? How do you mean?''

''I'm too quick to believe what people tell me,'' she replied. ''I just can't see Mr. Trefann and his wife being anything but what they say they are.''

''If she *is* his wife,'' I said.

''There you go again!'' she exclaimed. ''And why wouldn't she be, I'd like to know.''

''Where's her wedding ring?'' I asked. ''You saw for yourself she wears none. Yes, I know,'' I continued, knowing full well what her reply would be. ''She said she'd forgotten it at home. Which she very well may have done. On the other hand, if you'll pardon the pun, it could be quite a different story. Let's say, for the sake of argument,'' I carried on, ''that Mr. Trefann brings a female accomplice along with him as part of his cover when he signs in. A postman and his wife down on a holiday from London, if you please. Unfortunately, it never occurs to either one of them until it's too late that his lady friend wears no wedding ring. So a story is invented about her leaving it at home in a moment of forgetfulness.''

Violet shook her head in a show of resigned frustration. "There, you see," she said, "I'd never have thought of that. Maybe I'm not cut out for all this 'ere detecting business.''

"Stuff and nonsense, Mrs. Warner. Stuff and nonsense. Why," I said in an attempt to massage her deflated ego, "I wouldn't know what to do without you. I know what'll set things right," I told her. "A nice cup of tea. Mind, it *is* getting on," I added on rising, "but perhaps we can still round ourselves up a cup if the kitchen's still open." My companion readily agreed to the idea and, as I set about replacing the pillows back on the bed, took her stance by the door. "All set," I said, after giving one last pat to my hair in the mirror. At that, Vi opened the door and, as she did, let out a gasp.

"Mrs. Trefann!" she exclaimed. "Gave me a bit of a fright, you did.''

"Oh, I'm so sorry, Mrs. Warner," I heard the woman apologize. "I was just about to knock when you opened the door.''

" 'Ere," said Vi, "there's nothing wrong, is there?''

"Wrong? No, no, not at all," she said. "I thought I'd just pop by and see whether you'd care to join me in a game of cribbage downstairs. That is, if you have the time.''

"No, not tonight, luv, I'm afraid," replied Vi.

"Perhaps Mrs. Hudson, then?" she asked, peering round the door into the room.

"Actually, Mrs. Trefann," I announced, stepping forward into her view, "Mrs. Warner and I were just on our way downstairs to see about a cup of tea.''

"Oh, I see. Yes, well, I won't keep you," she replied with a smile. "Perhaps some other time then.''

"Aye, we'll make it another night, luv," stated Violet. "But thanks ever so for asking.''

"If you should change your mind," added Mrs. Trefann, before taking her leave, "you'll find me downstairs in the reading room."

Vi closed the door and turned her attention back to me. "Speak of the devil!" she exclaimed. "Here we were just talking about her and she shows up, nice as you please, at our door."

Whether her showing up when she did was a coincidence or not, I had no idea. My concern, as I mentioned to Vi, was just how long she'd been standing there. And whether she had heard any or all of what we'd been saying.

"Oh," said Vi, "I never thought of that. Well, I suppose we'll never know, will we?"

"No," I answered, "I suppose not. Then again . . . I wonder? Here, let's try a little experiment, shall we? Come, sit yourself down again," I said, ushering her back into her chair.

"What's all this about, eh?" she asked, sitting herself down and offering up a puzzled look.

"What I'm going to do," I explained, "is to stand outside the door. When I do, I want you to start talking in your normal voice. I'm going to try to see if I can hear what you're saying."

"What'll I say?"

"You can say anything you like," I replied.

"Oh, I know," she said. "I could recite—"

"Vi!" I cut in. "Don't tell me what you're going to say. If I know that, what would be the point?"

"Oh. Right."

I took my stance outside the door, waiting no more than a minute before reentering.

"Well," she asked, "could you hear anything?"

"No, not really," I confessed. "Only a word or two here and there, at best."

"Ah, well," she smiled, "that's all right then, isn't it."

"That," I said, "would depend on what words they were that she heard. But enough of this for now, m'girl," I announced, flinging open the door. "Let's see about getting ourselves some tea, shall we?"

TEN

The Face on Page One

By MID-AFTERNOON OF the following day, after having once again mulled over what I knew about our fellow guests and, in the process, peeling away like so many onion skins layers of accumulated information, I believed I had narrowed our list of suspects down to two. Which of the two it was could only be determined by my seeking out answers at two very different locations.

Since I would be out for the better part of the afternoon, I also had in mind dropping in to see Inspector Radcliffe. I thought it only prudent on my part to bring him into the picture as I saw it. What his reaction would be, I had no idea. But if it came to pass that I should find myself in the position of requiring his assistance at a moment's notice, his response would be swift if he had a better understanding of the situation. At least that was my hope.

I slipped into my coat, put on my hat, and, in seeking out Violet, found her seated in the reading room leafing through a magazine. "Ah, there you are," I said, taking myself over to her. "I've been looking for you."

"Looking for me?" she repeated, setting the magazine

aside. "Why, what have *I* done? And 'ere," she added, eyeing my coat and hat, "where are you off to, eh?"

"It's not what you've done," I replied in a smile. "It's what I'd like you to do. As to the coat and hat, I'm off to the constabulary to see the inspector, for one thing. As well as one or two other places. I thought that perhaps you might want to come along."

"The inspector!" she exclaimed. "Why, whatever's happened now?"

"Nothing at all," I assured her. "I just thought we should fill him in on what we believe is going on around here. I'll wait here," I added, "while you get your coat." Violet made no move and looked a little uncomfortable, I thought, in answering that if it was all the same to me, she'd pass on the idea. Her response took me aback to the extent that I asked if she was losing interest in the case.

"No, it's not that," she hedged. "It's just—just that Mrs. Trefann asked me this morning if I'd join her in a game of cards this afternoon. She'll be along any minute now, like as not."

"Mrs. Trefann?"

"Aye," she answered. "Seems her hubby's taken to his bed what with him being a bit under the weather like. So she's on her own for the rest of the day."

Being surprised and, yes, I'll admit, somewhat hurt as well by her refusal of my request, I curtly informed her that if that was her wish, so be it.

"Oh, now, Em," she responded in an attempt to mollify me, "there's no need to be getting yourself all upset. I'd love to go, I would, but not today. Thing is, we *are* on a holiday. Don't want to be spending every day 'ere running down clues or whatnot, do we? Where you're off to can wait till tomorrow, can't it?"

"Unfortunately, no," I answered. "Not when we're this close." Although, having said that, I could well understand her reason for declining to accompany me. Lord knows we both were more than entitled to a day off from our so-called holiday. For to be perfectly honest, there was a part of me that would have loved to have chucked it all then and there and taken the next train back to London. But I had picked up the scent, as it were, and was equally as anxious to run it down. As for Violet, I told her that I understood her need for a respite from the case and, that while I would have preferred her company, there was no absolute need for her to accompany me. "But one thing does bother me," I added. "This game of yours with Mrs. Trefann—do you think that's wise? She *is* a suspect, you know."

"Oh, no need for you to go worrying on that score," she assured me. "I'll keep me mouth shut 'bout you know what."

"I should hope so," I replied, before asking if she could do me a favor.

"Aye. What's that then?"

"Check with Mr. Burbage, would you, to see if Mr. Jones has left a letter with him within the last day or so to be mailed to London."

"In other words," she answered with a knowing smile, "to find out just whether this mysterious wife of his really exists. Right? But," she added, "I don't think Burbage would tell me if Jones had left it with him or not, would he?"

"You might put it to him," I suggested, "that Mr. Jones has asked you to see whether the letter he left with him to be mailed the other day had got away safely or not."

"But what if Burbage says there weren't no letter left with him?" she quizzed. "Does that mean Jones is—?"

"It could mean a number of things," I said. "In any event, let's wait, shall we, and see just what Mr. Burbage has to say. As for now," I stated, "I'd best get a move on. Enjoy your game then, luv. And I'll see you in time for supper."

"Mrs. Hudson, Inspector," announced Sergeant Styles on opening the door for me as I entered the man's office. Inspector Radcliffe rose from his desk. "Mrs. Hudson, this is a surprise," he said, acknowledging my presence with a welcoming smile. "Come in. Sit yourself down," he added, beckoning me to the chair in front of his desk. I offered up a greeting in return and sat myself down as the sergeant retreated to the outer office.

"Now then," spoke the inspector, "to what do I owe this honor? Nothing serious, is it, I trust?"

"As to the seriousness of it, Inspector," I replied, "I'll leave that for you to decide."

"You make it sound as if you've some sort of mystery on your hands, ma'am."

"As I still have a number of questions left unanswered," I said, "I would have to answer that I do indeed, as you say, have a mystery on my hands."

"This mystery of yours wouldn't have anything to do with the death of Mr. Latham, now would it?" he asked while still retaining his smile.

"Actually," I replied, "that's part of it, yes."

His smile disappeared. "Oh, come now, Mrs. Hudson," he admonished me. "I would have thought better of you than that. The man took a tumble in a darkened attic and fell, striking his head. These things happen. I'm afraid, dear lady, you're reading more into this than needs be."

"Mr. Latham," I informed him, "is but a part of the overall picture."

"Is he indeed?" His response was accompanied by a faint smirk which he did nothing to hide. "I would have thought he'd be the end of it. And what exactly is this overall picture of which you speak?"

"By way of explanation, Inspector," I replied, "I should like to begin with a crime I know you are all too familiar with."

"Oh, yes? And what one would that be?"

"The theft of the Star of Hyderabad from the Windermere estate," I answered. To say I had caught him completely off-guard would be an understatement.

"The Hyderabad theft!" he sputtered. "Now I *am* confused. "What in the world has that got to do with Latham's death? Please, Mrs. Hudson," he added in a most condescending fashion, "one crime at a time, if you please."

"But my dear Inspector," I countered, "that's just my point. I believe the theft, as well as Mr. Latham's death and all the other strange occurrences that have taken place within the last week, are intertwined within the same puzzle."

The man looked clearly annoyed. "In the first place," he said, "I wasn't aware there *was* a puzzle. And in the second place," he continued as his eyes locked with mine, "if you can tell me how a missing diamond and a man's accidental death in an attic are, as you say, intertwined, I shall be very much surprised. Very much surprised indeed."

Inspector Radcliffe, I thought, was going to be a hard man to convince. Still, the fact that he was willing to listen was something at least. I then began by taking him back to the time of the Windermere theft and continued on from there right up to the night of our midnight encounter with the coach and four. When I had finished, he sat back in his chair and studied me most thoroughly.

"I'll say this for you, Mrs. Hudson," he spoke at last, "you've built yourself a house full of information. Information," he added, "that I find most intriguing."

"Why, thank you, Inspector," I replied, feeling more than a little pleased with myself.

"Unfortunately," he said, "it's a house without a foundation."

Oh, dear, that didn't sound too good. "I'm afraid I don't understand," I said.

"You tell me an interesting tale but offer up no proof, ma'am. You say," he continued, resting his elbows on the desk as he leaned forward, "one of your fellow lodgers over at Burbage's is responsible for Dobbs's and Latham's death. Proof? None. You say the Star of Hyderabad lies hidden somewhere within the attic. Proof? None. You also say this murderer of yours is now masquerading as the ghost of Captain Hammond. Proof? None."

I did so wish he'd stop saying that. "But Inspector," I

countered, "our so-called ghost has been seen on various occasions by a number of guests within the house."

"Has he indeed, Mrs. Hudson? I wonder. As you know, I'm well aware of the validity of eyewitness accounts as to what they've seen or what they think they have seen," he said, no doubt in reference to those at the pub where Dobbs was last seen with his murderer.

"And what of the note Mrs. Warner and I received under our door and the coach that tried to run us down?" I asked, becoming a trifle miffed at his habit of airily brushing aside aspects of the case as they were presented to him.

"The note? A prank—a practical joke, no doubt. The coach? I believe you mentioned it was Mrs. Warner herself who first thought it was the work of some drunken driver, was it not?"

I nodded that it was.

"Well," he said, sitting back in his chair with self-satisfaction written all over his face, "there you are, you see. All neat and tidy."

"If that's the way you see it, Inspector," I said, "all well and good." I was neither upset nor angry. For, as I explained to him, I had done my duty as I saw it by informing him of all that I knew, believed, and surmised with respect to both the theft of the gem as well as the subsequent murders of Messrs Dobbs and Latham.

"And don't think I'm not appreciative of all you've told me, Mrs. Hudson," he assured me. "Although, as you can well understand, I'm sure, that without any evidence to go on, I can offer you no official assistance."

"Nor do I seek it," I answered. "At least not at this point. However, there may come a time—"

"Should such an occasion present itself," he answered with a smile on rising to his feet, "you've but to let me know." I rose from my chair. We shook hands across the desk as I thanked him for the opportunity of hearing me out. "No need to go thanking me, Mrs. Hudson," he cheerfully responded. "My office is always open to you. And while I admit that our opinions may differ as to what did or didn't happen, you've given me food for thought, ma'am. I'll say that much.''

"I could ask for nothing more,'' I assured him.

"If you like,'' he added, walking me to the door, "I can have the sergeant see about giving you a lift back to Burbage House.''

"Why,'' I replied, "that's ever so kind of you, Inspector. But actually, I'm on my way over to the Brighton *Herald*.''

"The newspaper?''

"Yes, that's right. What I have in mind is digging through their back copies to search out what they have on the Windermere theft. I'm sure they'd still have it on file.''

"By gad, Mrs. Hudson,'' he chortled, "you never give up, do you? Would that my staff were as diligent. But here, hold on a minute.'' Leaving me at the door, he made his way over to his filing cabinet. Once there, he pulled out a drawer and leafed through its contents before at last removing a manila folder. This he placed on his desk and, after a quick perusal of one particular page, wrote something down on a slip of paper. "Here,'' he said, returning to me with it in his hand. "I've written down the day, month, and year of the robbery for you. It'll make it that much easier for them to find it for you when you get there.''

Needless to say I thanked him most profusely.

"Not at all,'' he answered with an airy wave of his hand. "Although,'' he added, "I don't know what you hope to find that you don't already know. Or what I've already told you, for that matter.''

I replied that I wasn't looking for any one thing in particular, but felt that in browsing through the newspaper's story on the robbery, it might help me get a better feel for the case, not having been there at the outset of it all.

"Again, Mrs. Hudson, I applaud your diligence,'' he said, on opening the door of his office for me and, in so doing, catching his sergeant gazing aimlessly out the window. "Oh, Styles,'' he called out, "drop Mrs. Hudson off at the *Herald*, would you?''

"Oh, really, Inspector," I protested, "there's no need for—"

"Nonsense, ma'am. The sergeant here will be only too happy to be doing something worthwhile. Eh, Styles?"

I again thanked the inspector and bade him a good day— what there was left of it. He responded in kind and stepped back into his office, closing the door behind him. As he did so, I turned my attention to his subordinate. "If you'd rather not," I said, "it's quite understandable. I can easily find my way over there by myself."

"Won't be no trouble at all, Mrs. Hudson," he answered. "Besides," he added with a grin, "I haven't all that much to do. 'Cept a bit of paperwork. Dull as dishwater around here, it is. If I do say so myself."

"That could all very well change, Sergeant," I replied a little too smugly. "Things could get very exciting around here for you yet."

"You mean about this here ghost business of yours?" he asked. "Who do you really think it is that's behind it all?"

I stopped in my tracks and gave him a most quizzical look.

"I wasn't standing by the window *all* the time," he responded with a wink. "And the inspector's door isn't all that thick."

"Then you know as much as I," I stated, adding that it was nice to see that I had at least one member of the force on my side.

"Oh, I believe you're onto something, all right," he assured me. "And oh, what wouldn't I give to be in on the solving of it. Wouldn't *that* ruffle the inspector's feathers!" he gleefully announced.

I too smiled at the thought of it. "I daresay it would," I answered. "But who knows? Perhaps you'll get a chance to play a part in it yet," I added as a measure of consolement, if nothing else. "The case is still open-ended."

"Humph!" he snorted. "Not likely. Not with the inspector keeping me under his thumb as he does. The way

I see it, I'm wasted here in Brighton, I am, Mrs. Hudson. And I don't mind telling you,'' he confided, ''there's been many the time I thought of applying for a position with Scotland Yard.''

''Why haven't you?'' I asked.

He made a face. ''Fat chance I'd have,'' he said.

I then made mention that I was acquainted with a certain Inspector Lestrade of the Yard. ''If you like,'' I said, ''I'll have a word with him on your behalf.''

The good sergeant was beside himself at the prospect and could not thank me enough. At least, I thought, I've made someone's day a little brighter. If nothing else.

After his procuring a horse and carriage from the police stables, we were on our way. ''By the bye, Sergeant,'' I asked as we continued on at a merry clip, ''you wouldn't by any chance happen to have a street map of London back at the station, would you? I should have thought to ask when I was there,'' I admitted, ''but it completely slipped my mind.''

He shook his head. ''Not back at the station, no, ma'am,'' he answered. ''But I believe my sister would. She and her husband took a trip there only last year. Their first one to London, it was. And if I'm not mistaken, I remember seeing it among the things they brought back with them.''

''Could you check?'' I asked. ''I'd be ever so grateful.''

''I can and will, Mrs. Hudson,'' he stated. ''And if she has, I'll pop it over to you first chance I get. Oh,'' he added, ''speaking of forgetting things, I know what it was I meant to tell you. When you get over to the *Herald*, ask for Mr. McGuire. He's the chap you'd want to see.''

I thanked him and made a mental note of the name. On our arrival, he offered to wait but I declined, stating that I had no idea how long I'd be. With that, he headed back to the station and I, in turn, entered the front door of the Brighton *Herald*.

''I'd like to see Mr. McGuire, if I may,'' I said, addressing a wispy-haired gentleman seated at a desk behind the front counter. He adjusted his eyeshade and looked up at me with an air of resigned weariness.

"Oh, would you now?" he said. "And what would you be wantin' with him?"

"I'm told he might be able to help," I answered. "I have the information here," I said, rummaging my hand around in the pocket of my coat. "Somewhere here," I mumbled feeling a little foolish as I delved a hand into the other pocket. "It's about the Windermere robbery," I stated by way of explanation.

"If it's a crime you're reporting," he remarked as I continued to fish about for the paper, "it's best you be seeing Mr. Tumpane. He's our police reporter."

"No, no," I hastened to inform him, "this robbery occurred a good many years ago. Ah," said I with a smile, on bringing forth the now-crumpled paper and handing it over to him. "Here's the information as to the date of it."

"Then it's a back issue you'd be wanting," he said, scanning the information the inspector had set down.

"Yes, that's right. I was told a Mr. McGuire would be the one to see. Is he in?"

"It's himself you're looking at," he replied.

"You're Mr. McGuire?"

"I am that."

We seemed to be at some sort of an impasse. "Well then," I spoke at last, "is it possible to see a back copy?"

"I'd have to be going downstairs to get it," he grudgingly informed me. "Though it's not the going down I mind, it's the lugging of it back up. And what with me back being the way it is—"

"Lugging it?" Had I heard him right? "But surely," I questioned, "one newspaper can't be all that heavy—?"

"One newspaper, she says!" He rolled his eyes heavenward in mock anguish. "And aren't they all kept by consecutive years in ledgers? Big, heavy, leather-bound ledgers?"

"I've no idea," I answered. "Are they?"

"They are," he stated. "But I suppose you wouldn't be

asking to see it if it wasn't important to you." And, so saying, he raised himself up out of his chair and bade me wait 'til he returned. And return he did. Bearing with him, as he had so described, a large, heavy, leather-bound ledger. And with much huffing and puffing, he managed to set it down on the counter in front of me. After thanking him for his trouble, I was left alone to peruse the pages.

I began by eagerly skimming through the yellowing sheets 'til at last coming upon the edition in question. There it was, in a banner headline. DIAMOND THEFT AT WINDERMERE! THIEF CAUGHT! I scanned the article and, while it did offer up hitherto unknown information, I found it to be of dubious value. However, what did capture my attention were the accompanying photographs of those involved. They were all there, including Inspector Grimes who was at that time in charge of the case and a then-Sergeant Radcliffe, looking very serious and a good ten years younger. Also, Charlie Allbright himself, along with Lord and Lady Ashcroft, the maid Annie, and other members of the household staff. Faces that for the most part had been no more than names to me but a moment ago. On the bottom half of the page was an illustration of the Star of Hyderabad. And though it was in black and white, it fair took my breath away.

With one last glance at the gallery of faces staring back at me, I was about to turn the page but stopped in the realization that one face in particular looked vaguely familiar. I took a closer look. Even allowing for a ten-year passage in time, I told myself, it could have been none other.

In a state of excitement, I hastily closed the ledger, offered up my thanks to Mr. McGuire, and away I went. My second stop that I had planned could wait until tomorrow. I was anxious to return to my room where I could take the time out to better evaluate this new dimension to the case. Besides that, I was famished, and supper awaited me.

*　　*　　*

On my arrival back at Burbage's, I opened the front door, stepped inside, and caught the aroma of food wafting its way into the hall. I peeked round into the dining room and saw that Violet had already taken herself down to dinner. Catching her eye, I smiled and held up one finger to indicate I'd be but a minute in joining her. Then it was up the staircase for me and back to our room.

After removing my coat and hat I pondered as to whether or not a change of dress was in order. A quick glance into the dresser mirror convinced me I looked presentable enough as I was. Besides, I was anxious to return downstairs to announce to Vi what I had discovered at the newspaper office. It was then I began to have second thoughts as to just how wise that would be. One wrong word or a slip of the tongue from Vi to anyone, however unintentional it would be, was the last thing I needed at this stage of the game. No, it was best that I kept what I knew to myself. At least for the present.

After one last look in the mirror I was all set. Although, to be honest, my hair could have stood a bit of grooming. Should I bother? Ah, well, for all the time it would take, I told myself, why not? My hairbrush lay but an arm's length away on the dresser top. As I reached out for it, my hand stopped in midair. For I thought I had seen the brush move ever so slightly. I shook my head and blinked my eyes, not knowing quite what to think. Perhaps I had imagined it. Yes, that was it. Those tired old eyes of mine were playing tricks on—no, there, it moved again! This time, sliding back and forth at an accelerated rate of speed across the top of the dresser before at last falling to the floor. As it did, the room was engulfed in an unearthly chill. I now knew all too well the full meaning of it.

"You're here, aren't you, Mrs. Hammond?" I said, addressing myself to the unseen presence. No answer. Nothing. The room was as still as death itself. "Mrs. Hammond," I again called out, not really expecting an answer. In truth, I didn't know quite what to expect. Was I apprehensive? Yes. Frightened? Yes. But not to the extent

I had been on my first encounter with the lady from the great beyond. My eyes searched the room but saw nothing. But wait, over there by the corner near the window. Something. Yes, I could see it better now. A small pinpoint of light. I stood in awed silence, watching it spread itself out ever larger until it engulfed the entire corner of the room. Within that circle of light a human form began to take shape. It was the figure of a woman. That woman was Sarah Hammond. As she became more and more visible to me, the light began to fade into nothingness until it was no more. Although she appeared as three-dimensional, I found it odd that I could still see through her, as it were. It was all rather disconcerting.

She remained standing where she was with head bowed and hands clasped in front of her. The silence between the two of us was unbearable. Slowly she raised her head and, when she did, those dead, vacant eyes met mine. "You must leave this house," she said. Her voice had a hollowness to it and was barely above a whisper.

"But Mrs. Hammond," I replied, gathering up my courage, "this is no longer a private home. If I could just make you—"

She raised her hand in a gesture for silence. "Take heed of what I say, madam. This I tell you for your own good," she added in a voice that implied no threat on her part.

Take heed? I didn't understand. "Do you see me as being in some sort of danger?" I asked. "Is that why you seek me out? To warn me?" I received no answer.

"You are a good woman," she spoke at last.

While flattered, it was not the response I sought. "I thank you for thinking so," I answered. "But as to my question—"

"Must go. Must go now," she interjected with much wringing of hands. "Must find John. Much work to be done. House in need of repair. John. John." Her voice began fading away in tandem with her spiritual self.

"No, wait, please," I cried out. But she was gone.

I sat myself down on the bed, much shaken by the experience. What was I to make of it? Had she appeared merely to state her objection to my presence in a house she still believed was hers? If that were so, why me, and not the others? Did she perceive me as being some sort of a threat? No, I told myself, that can't be right. A good woman, she had called me. Was it a warning then on my behalf? Had she peered into the future and witnessed my demise? Would that I could ask Mr. Latham if he too had been the recipient of such a warning from the lady. If so, it was one he had obviously chosen to ignore. I must be very careful, I told myself, not to make the same mistake.

As for supper, I was afraid I had to forego it. My encounter with the vaporous Sarah Hammond had left me with a sudden and decided loss of appetite. But, knowing Vi would wonder as to what was keeping me, I thought it best to take myself down to the dining room. On joining her at our table I waved aside any suggestion of supper and settled instead for tea. It was only after much urging from my companion did I make an attempt at spooning down a few mouthfuls of a cinnamon-sprinkled custard.

"Off your feed then, are you, luv?" she asked in a show of concern. "Pale as death, you are. Why," she said, "if I didn't know better, I'd say you looked as if you'd just seen—" She stopped short in the realization that indeed I had. " 'Ere!" she blurted out. "Not Sarah again!"

I cautioned her to silence on noticing her outburst had resulted in a few eyebrows being raised from the adjoining tables. One table in particular caught my attention. Mr. Christie, I noted, continued to dine alone. What was the reason given for his wife's absence? Ah, yes, an urgent family matter. Evidently she would not be returning.

"Well, go on then," whispered Vi. "What happened with you know who, eh?"

I put forward the suggestion that it might be best if we continued our conversation upstairs.

"Aye, right you are then, luv," she agreed. "I'll just finish off that custard of yours, if you like, 'fore we go. No sense wastin' it."

Once back in our room I found it hard to believe that such a ghostly visitation had actually occurred. Yet there on the floor lay proof enough that it had. I bent down, picked up my hairbrush, and placed it back in its original position on top of the dresser. No sooner had I done so than I was bombarded with questions from Vi as to the captain's wife. Where had I seen her? When did I see her? Did she say anything to me? And so on and so forth. As calmly as I could, I related in detail all that I had said, seen, felt, and experienced. Including the woman's words in regard to my vacating the premises.

"Trying to warn you, that's what she were trying to do, all right," announced Violet. "They say that spirits can see things that are going to happen before they do. And if you recall, Emma Hudson," she reminded me with a wag of her finger in my direction, "that there Madame Zerina told you more or less the same thing. If you ask me," she added most adamantly, "I say we clear out of 'ere first thing tomorrow morning."

I should at this point explain Vi's reference to a certain Madame Zerina. I have not done so before due to an unwillingness on my part to appear foolish in admitting that Madame Zerina was, as the name no doubt implies, for all intents and purposes a fortune-teller. And that both Violet and I had availed ourselves of her services. As I say, I only speak of it now due to Vi's mentioning her name, plus the fact that what the woman in question had told me at the time coincided in some measure with Sarah Hammond's words of warning.

It all began during our trip down to the piers on the day we had dropped into Christie's fish and chip shop. A sign inside the window of an adjoining tea shop had caught Vi's eye. "Oh, look, Em," was my companion's delighted response, "it says 'Private readings available to one and all by the world-famous Madame Zerina.' What do you think?"

"World-famous?" I questioned with a smile. "I've never heard of her."

"No," she said, "I mean, what do you think 'bout us going in and having our fortune read, eh?"

I responded in a lighthearted way by questioning whether she really believed in that sort of thing.

"Well, 'course I do," she stated, stoutly defending her position. "Mean to tell me you don't?"

"Oh, I've no doubt," I answered, "that there are those who, by whatever means, can at times catch a glimpse of the future. As a matter of fact," I continued, "I recall a maiden aunt of mine who, on those occasions when she'd come a-calling, would read both mine and my mother's fortune from the tea leaves in our cups. Without accepting so much as a farthing for her services. Or gift, as she called it."

"Well, then," quizzed Vi, "what are you saying, then?"

"What I'm saying," I informed her, "is that it's best to beware of those who do it for a livelihood. And," I added, "who bill themselves as being world-famous."

"Oh, Em," said she, "don't be such an old stick-in-the-mud. Come on," I was urged with a tug to my sleeve. "It'll be a giggle, like."

Perhaps she was right. After all, we *were* supposed to be on a holiday. I shrugged my shoulders in acquiescence and followed her in.

Save for ourselves, the place was empty. Faded, red-checkered tablecloths hung down dejectedly over small circular tables set in no particular arrangement within the room. It was to one of these tables, placed beside a curtained cubicle in the corner, that we settled ourselves down. It was but a minute later that we caught the sound of a beaded curtain that served as a door in back being parted. Through it came an old crone of a woman wearing an outlandish red bandana on her head with naught but the bottom of her earlobes being visible from beneath it. From each of those lobes hung a silver chain bearing three enormous gold stars that clinked-clanked with every step she took toward us.

"Come in to have your fortunes read then, have you,

dearies?'' she questioned with a gap-toothed smile. I nodded in the affirmative and, on returning her smile, could
not help but notice that her elongated nose carried a decidedly large blemished protuberance to the side of it. Which,
for some reason or the other, led me to wonder if her vision
encompassed a wart's eye view of the world. ''What'll it
be then?'' she asked. ''Tea leaves, crystal ball, tarot—''

''Oh,'' beamed Vi. ''A crystal ball! That sounds ever so
exciting.''

''Right,'' she said. ''Come along then, dearie. Into me
private quarters,'' she added with a cackle on leading Vi
into the cloth-enclosed cubicle.

With the two of them now inside, I began to have second
thoughts as to whether or not I should bother having my
fortune read as well. I had been through this sort of thing
before and considered it a waste of time.

''First you must cross my palm with silver,'' spoke Madame Zerina.

''Silver?'' questioned Vi. '' 'Ere, what would I be doing
with silver?''

This was ridiculous. Private quarters, indeed! I could
hear every word being said.

''The money, dearie. The money,'' announced the old
crone in some annoyance. ''My fee. Now then, just give
me a minute to concentrate,'' she continued, after the
exchange had taken place. ''There,'' she said, ''the ball is
becoming less cloudy now. I'm seeing you as having trav-
eled a great distance to be here.''

Easy enough, I thought, since those who wandered in
would be largely tourists.

''Well, it weren't all that great a distance,'' announced
an all too innocent Vi. ''We're down here from London.
But I'm originally from Manchester.''

I threw up my hands in despair. Give Violet enough time,
I told myself, and she'll end up telling her our whole life
story.

''London, yes, that's right,'' confirmed the seer, after Vi

had established as much. "But you left Manchester to go to London, right?"

"Aye, that's right."

"Yes, I see that you did," she answered. "It's all here," she cackled, no doubt indicating the crystal ball. "But wait!" she exclaimed. "I see someone. A face is coming through. Someone who's passed over. A man."

"Why," said Vi, "it must be my Bert."

"Was he ever called Albert?" she quizzed.

Oh, this was too much. What would he have been called—George?

"Aye," announced Violet. "Albert was his Christian name."

"Yes, I thought so," replied the woman, all very knowingly. "He's showing me the letter A and saying, 'That's right. That's right.'"

"'Ere," spoke Vi, "I wonder why he just didn't tell you his name in the first place?"

"Do not question the spirits," my companion was promptly advised. "He's telling me," continued Madame Zerina after a slight pause, "that he's very happy and you are not to worry about him. And," she added, "that he's having a fine old time."

"And is Mr. Hudson with him then?" asked Violet.

"Mr.—?"

"Hudson," repeated Vi. "Em's husband. The lady waiting outside."

There she goes again, I thought.

"Yes, yes, you're right," was the old crone's sudden confirmation. "There *is* another man there. I see him now. They have their arms around each other's shoulders. They're singing a song. They liked to sing, didn't they."

"Not that I remember," admitted Vi.

"Well, they're singing now!" she was curtly informed. "Now then, dearie," continued the woman, who obviously felt a need for a change in subject, "about your health. I see no immediate problems. Though be careful," she added, "that you lift nothing heavy. I'm seeing that it could cause you back pain."

"I'll remember that," Violet dutifully informed her.

"Do you have any questions?" queried the old woman.

"Don't see anybody leaving me a fortune, do you?" she asked with a chuckle.

"I see you receiving a letter," Madame was all too quick to inform her. "It is from a barrister. Some sort of legal document. It could mean a great deal of money for you. I see it arriving by post within the next three months."

"Oh, lovely," responded Vi with a smile in her voice. "And you can see all that in that there crystal ball of yours, can you? Coo!"

And so it went in much the same vein until at last the old crone announced that the aforementioned crystal ball had clouded over and she could see no more.

After emerging from the cubicle and returning to our table Vi was, of course, ecstatic in proclaiming the woman's *psychic* abilities. In the state she was in, I knew it would only cause a scene between the two of us if I were to suddenly announce my intention of foregoing the dubious pleasure of having my fortune read as well. And so it was that I entered the cubicle, crossed the old crone's palm with 'silver,' and waited to hear what the gods (or Madame Zerina) had in store for me.

What she offered up was more or less a rehash of what I had already heard. Which didn't surprise me. What did surprise me was the uneasiness that she exhibited toward me. This I put down to my belief that Madame Zerina was well aware that a nonbeliever sat opposite her. When the session at last ended, I thankfully arose from my chair. But to my surprise, she bade me return to my seat. I did so questioningly.

"I'm an old woman," she announced. "And my powers are not what they once were. But what am I to do, eh, dearie? Got to live, haven't I? I could see you're a skeptic," she went on, while I wondered why on earth she was telling me all this. "And maybe," she admitted, "you've a right to be. But," she continued, "once in a while I still get what you might call a flash into the future."

"I don't understand. What exactly are you trying to tell me?" I asked.

"Be careful, dearie," she advised. It was advice complete with a bony finger being wagged in my face. "There's a heaviness surrounding you," she continued. "I felt it the moment you walked in. Ominous, it is. Not a good sign."

Good Lord, was the woman predicting my death? I screwed up my courage and asked her as much.

"I wouldn't say so even if I could," she answered. "I'll only say I see a real threat to you. If you pass through the next few days unharmed, all will be well. I'll say no more."

While I had been shaken and stunned by what I had heard, in time her message of warning had faded into the recesses of my mind. If I had thought of it at all since then, it was with a sense of bemusement. Now, I wasn't so sure.

"Oh, I'm sorry, Vi," I said, returning my attention back to my companion. "I'm afraid I drifted off in thought for a moment. What was it you were saying?"

"I said," she repeated, "we should clear out of 'ere first thing tomorrow morning."

"I'd agree with you," I replied, "if I didn't feel we're close to seeing an end to it all. By the way," I added, "did you speak to Mr. Burbage as to whether Mr. Jones had left a letter with him to be posted?"

"Oh, aye," she replied. "Had a chance to speak to him just before going in for supper."

"And he told you," I answered all too knowingly, "that indeed such a letter had been left in his care by Mr. Jones. Right?"

"Why, Em," replied Vi, "you couldn't be more wrong if you wanted to be."

"What!" I exclaimed. "Are you saying—"

"I'm saying," she announced, "that according to Burbage, Jones didn't leave no letter with him to be posted. The only letters left with him were from the Trefanns."

"The Trefanns?"

"Aye. And they weren't really letters like. Only a couple of postcards."

"But," I pressed, "you're sure Jones left no letter."

"Not from what Burbage says, he didn't."

Her news stunned me. I sat myself down to puzzle over what I had heard. If Jones had lied about sending off a letter, what else had he lied about? I had had two prime suspects in mind when entering the newspaper office earlier that day, Mr. Jones being one of the two. On leaving it with my newfound knowledge, Mr. Jones was no longer on my list. But now, having caught him in a lie—Had I been too quick in absolving him as being our Captain Hammond? This would take some rethinking on my part. But not tonight.

"So," said Vi, "where does that leave us with Jones then?"

"Ask me tomorrow, Vi," I answered. "When my mind is clearer."

"But what about the inspector then?" she questioned. "Got a chance to get over to see him, did you?"

I assured her that I had, adding that he seemed quite interested, if not intrigued, by all I had told him. "Mind you," I continued, "it may very well be he was merely expressing interest as a way of placating me. In any event, I believe we at least have an ally in Sergeant Styles. But what about you?" I quizzed. "How went your card game with Mrs. Trefann?"

Vi's face registered disgust. "If you ask me," she said, "she weren't no card player. We eventually ended up playing Old Maid, would you believe? Even at that, I beat her four games out of five."

"How long did all this take?" I asked.

"Better part of an hour. Maybe more. Seemed like more," she added with a snicker. "Glad to see the end of it, I was."

"And you didn't say anything about what we've—"

" 'Ere, not a word!" was the haughty response. "Know

better than that, I do. Mind, we didn't sit there like a couple of bumps on a log. She did ask what I thought of Mrs. Christie's absence and whether I'd come across the captain's ghost again."

"And you said?"

"I said as how we thought the Christies had some sort of a row and that she'd up and left him. And no, I told her, I hadn't seen the captain. 'Once was enough,' I says, 'thank you very much.' "

"And she," I asked, "has only seen Sarah Hammond the once?"

"So she said."

"And Mrs. Trefann's husband," I continued, "never did manage to put in an appearance during this card game of yours. Is that right?"

"Never seen hide nor hair of him," she replied. "Well, like she said, he'd taken to his bed. What with him being under the weather, like."

"And when you finally returned to our room," I quizzed, "was everything the way it should be?"

"Howd' you mean?"

"I mean, did anything look as if it had been moved about in any way?"

"Not that I noticed. Why," she quipped, "think Sarah might have floated in to throw the odd hairbrush around, do you?"

"It wasn't Sarah I had in mind," I answered, and let it go at that.

"Well," said she, on rising, "I don't know about you, Em, but I'm going to slip into me housecoat. This 'ere corset of mine is killing me. 'Less you were thinking of going downstairs," she added, "and wanted company."

"No, no," I announced. "You go right ahead. In fact, I think I'll get into mine as well." After having freed ourselves from the confines of our whalebone corsets (with grateful sighs of relief, I might add) and donned more comfortable bedroom garb, Vi made mention of having seen one of Doctor Watson's books in the reading room. "Oh, yes? And what one was that?" I asked.

"Hmmm," she said, pursing her lips in thought, "can't remember the name right off. Only saw it just before Mrs. Trefann arrived. *Studying*—something or other."

"*A Study in Scarlet?*"

"Aye. That were it. Thought it would be summat to read tomorrow. I would have brought it up with me tonight," she added, "but the light's not all that good in 'ere to read, is it? Now, what did I do with me other slipper?" she asked herself scanning the room. "Couldn't have walked off on its own. Read it then, have you?" she asked, bending down and groping about with an arm under the bed for the missing slipper.

"What? *A Study in Scarlet?* Yes, though it was some time ago now," I answered. "In fact, I believe it was one of the first, if not *the* first of the doctor's chronicles regarding the exploits of Mr. Holmes."

"Ah, 'ere it is!" she announced triumphantly on bringing forth the slipper. "And you're mentioned in the book, are you?" she asked as I helped her to her feet.

"Once or twice," I answered. "But not by name. Simply as the landlady, as I recall."

"What! The landlady? Well, I like that, I do!" she stated. Which meant, of course, that she didn't like it at all. "Give the doctor a piece of my mind, I will, when we gets back. See if I don't."

"You'll do no such thing," I stated just as firmly. "It matters not a whit to me one way or the other."

"You're a strange one, you are, Emma Hudson," she sighed with a shake of her head. "You should take to this 'ere writing business yourself," she advised. "Set down all the cases we've solved just like the doctor does. That's what I'd do if I had the knack for it."

"Yes, well," I answered, more to placate her than with any real thought in mind at the time of actually doing so, "perhaps I will one of these days. When I'm old and grey," I added with a mischievous wink.

"Old and grey, you say? Best you get cracking on it first thing tomorrow then, luv."

I laughed aside her good-natured barb and reminded myself that if I had best get cracking on anything, it had better be the solving of our mystery. But I could do nothing now but wait 'til the morrow.

We had taken to our bed earlier than usual that night and, after much tossing and turning about, I eventually drifted off. Albeit into a fitful sleep. Needless to say, it didn't help in being awakened at some time during the night by once again hearing a thumping about from the attic. "Please, Lord," I remember pleading drowsily, "please don't let him find the ring tonight. Give me one more day."

ELEVEN

Third Finger, Left Hand

⟨⟩ THE RAIN THAT had continued on and off
the following day had the effect of keeping everyone indoors. Shortly after lunch I noticed on passing by the reading room that Peter Jones had taken himself a chair by the
fire. Mrs. Trefann and her husband, who had obviously recovered from whatever it was that had ailed him yesterday,
were engaged in a game of cards, though showing little
enthusiasm for it. Like children kept inside on a rainy day
they were, as were we all, I suppose, trying to make the
best of it. As for Mrs. Burbage, the lady continued to scurry
about from room to room and, in the process, managing to
make herself look frightfully important. Which, I suppose,
was the whole purpose of it. For his part, Mr. Burbage
remained lost to the world with his head buried in a magazine behind the registration desk. Mr. Christie headed back
upstairs, as did Vi and I.

"Rain seems to be easin' up a bit," announced Violet,
on parting the curtained window of our room for a look-
see. "Maybe we've seen the last of it."

"Hard to tell," I replied. "It seems to come and go."

"Aye, true enough," she agreed. "And speaking of coming and going," she added, letting the curtain fall back into place as she turned to me, "what time is it we check out tomorrow morning?"

"Eleven o'clock, I believe," I answered.

"Counting the hours, I am," she stated in no uncertain terms. "This whole trip has been a disappointment, it has. In more ways than one, and no mistake."

"More ways than one?"

"Well," she said, "aside from the weather, I would have liked to have seen us solve all this ghost business 'fore we left. But," she added in a dejected, if not defeated, sigh, "it looks as if we've come a cropper on this one, luv."

"Look on the bright side of it," I replied, mustering up a smile. "We still have a day and a half left. Anything can happen yet."

"Day and a half, she says," mumbled Vi. "Half of this day's gone already. 'Sides," she said, "what do you hope to find out before checkout time that you don't know now?"

I offered up no answer.

" 'Ere now," said she, giving me the fish-eye, "you're not thinking of staying on now, are you?"

"I don't know," I replied honestly. "I hadn't really thought about it. Although, unlike ourselves," I continued, as the idea began to take hold, "I believe the others have booked their stay for a fortnight. Which means they'd be here for another week yet. I don't suppose there'd be any problem in our signing in for another seven days. It's not as if the Burbages had no vacancies."

"Well, if that's what you're thinking, Emma Hudson," stated a visibly upset Violet Warner, "you can count me out! What with horses trying to trample us underfoot and ghosts floatin' about and all," she continued in much the same agitated manner, "I've had me fill of it, I have."

"Oh, Vi," I reasoned, "there's no sense in getting yourself all upset. Let's just see what happens, shall we? It's just that I'd hate to leave Burbage House with the mystery still unsolved. You can understand that, can't you?''

"Aye. As would I, if it comes to that," she admitted. "But even Mr. Holmes doesn't solve every case," she declared. "*We* know that. 'Course the doctor never writes about those, does he?"

"Nor can I see any reason why he should," I responded. "Why write about a murder investigation that was left unsolved? It would be a disservice to the reader. And while we're on the subject of Doctor Watson," I added, "I thought you had in mind reading his *Study in Scarlet* this afternoon."

"Aye, that's right, I was," she said. "Might's well pop down now. It'll give me summat to do. You don't mind, do you, luv?"

"No, no, not at all," I assured her, adding that I'd probably be joining her later on. When she had taken her leave, I was left with a twinge of guilt for not mentioning to her the little trip I had in mind for myself. If I had spoken to her about it, I knew only too well she would have made a great to-do about wanting to accompany me. When, in truth, her preference would have been to stay indoors on such a day, as would I. But fair weather or foul, I knew it was something I couldn't put off.

No more than twenty minutes later I had slipped into my coat and hat, picked up my trusty umbrella, closed the door behind me, and stepped out into the hall. No sooner had I done so than who should I see but Mrs. Burbage advancing down the hallway bearing an armful of linen.

"Why, Mrs. Hudson," exclaimed the woman, "surely you're not going out on a day such as this?"

"I thought it was clearing up somewhat," was my feeble reply. At that moment a boom of thunder reverberated throughout the heavens. "Obviously not," I added, managing a weak smile. I thought that would be an end to it but she paused before me, expecting, I suppose, some sort of answer. What to say? "The . . . ah, chemist, you see," I at last replied.

"Pardon?"

"The chemist," I repeated. "Yes, that's it. I have a pre-scription, you see, that needs refilling." A plausible enough story, I thought. Evidently, Mrs. Burbage must have thought so as well. For she gave me the name of a chemist shop that, she informed me, was no more than a block away. I thanked her and, before continuing on my way down the hall, thought to ask her if she had heard any more in regard to Mrs. Christie's absence.

"Mrs. Christie?" Her reaction was either one of surprise or suspicion. It was hard to tell. "No," she answered, "nei-ther I nor Mr. Burbage know any more than what we've been told by that lady's husband. As I mentioned to you earlier, Mrs. Hudson," she continued, this time a little more testily, "in this business, people come and go at will for whatever the reason. But why all this interest in Mrs. Chris-tie, if I may ask?"

"Yes, well, it's just that when speaking to her previous to her sudden departure, I had found her to be a rather pleasant young woman," I answered, in the hope that the explanation would suffice.

"Did you indeed?" she questioned with arched eye-brows—and let it go at that.

It was clear that Mrs. Burbage, from what I knew of her, would have considered Liza Christie to have been a rather common young woman. As perhaps she was. Still, not even the proper Mrs. Burbage would have openly admitted as much to myself or to any other paying guest. And so it was that off I went, down the stairs and out the door, being careful as I passed the reading room not to let Vi see me.

In no more than an hour I was back. With the good news being that I was simply ecstatic over what I had learned. The bad news being that I was completely soaked. My um-brella, for whatever the reason, had failed to open. My hat and hair were a mess. Wet and bedraggled, I paused long enough in the lobby for a peek into the reading room. The Trefanns, I noted, remained busily engaged in their game of cards. From what I could see, Vi had found the doctor's book to her liking. For she appeared deeply engrossed in

the story. If it had been the Baker Street parlor, I would
not have hesitated a moment in rushing in with my news.
As it was, it would have to wait until she had taken herself
back upstairs. Whether Mr. Jones remained at his place by
the fire, I took no time to notice. My one thought being to
make it up to our room as quickly as possible in order to
dry out and freshen up. Looking the way I did, I was thankful that Mr. Burbage was nowhere to be seen as I ascended
the stairs.

Once back inside our room, I set aside my umbrella,
placed my hat on the dresser, draped my wet coat over the
back of one chair, and settled myself down on the other.
And there I sat, feeling quite pleased with myself, as well
I should have. For I now knew beyond a shadow of a doubt
(as the courts are wont to say) just who our mysterious,
murdering Captain Hammond really was. The question remaining now, however, was how to prove it. Proof, Mrs.
Hudson, proof. As the inspector is also wont to say. Had I
actually seen him bring the rock down on the head of Mr.
Dobbs? I could hear him ask. Was I there to see him strike
the fatal blow that resulted in the death of Mr. Latham?
Had I actually confronted him in the garb of the late Captain Hammond? To all those questions I would, of course,
have had to answer no. But it could have been no other.
Of that I was sure. That's what made it all so frustrating.
Ah, but if I could catch him in the act of retrieving the
gem, perhaps—then? But what chance would I have of
that?

And what of this Star of Hyderabad, I pondered. Its place
of hiding must have been quite ingenious indeed. For even
our so-called ghost, rummaging about the attic as he had
been, night after night, had been unable to unearth its location. One would think, I told myself, the fact that its place
of concealment made it impossible to locate meant that
Charlie Allbright had had ample time in which to devise a
foolproof hiding place. But he hadn't. Nor would he have
any reason for doing so. He was arrested the day after the
robbery. Which meant he would have had only the one

night at Burbage's to sneak it up to the attic and squirrel it away. He had no reason to believe he'd be caught. The hiding of it was simply an extra precaution on his part.

I mentally pictured him coming up to the attic, taking a quick look around, spotting a site for it, and leaving it there. Then he takes off back down the stairs to his room before you can say, "Bob's your uncle." All of which, if true, meant that its place of hiding must be a fairly obvious one. Then why hadn't the ring ever been found?

The ring. Something clicked in my mind at the thought of it. But what? Had I seen a ring somewhere, or—? No, I suddenly remembered it wasn't a ring I had seen, but one I hadn't. It was Mrs. Trefann's wedding ring I'd been thinking of, that was it. Having, as she said, left it at home in a moment of forgetfulness.

For my part, this wedding band of mine had never been taken off since William had slipped it on my finger on that day of days so many years ago. I gazed down lovingly at it and gently rubbed my finger over it. And, in doing so, it was as if I had rubbed Aladdin's lamp. For although no genie appeared before me, a thought just as startling did. The wedding band—of course! That was it! It had to be. The idea of where he had put the ring struck me as so amusing that I laughed out loud at the thought of it. Charlie Allbright, it seemed, had a delicious, but hitherto unknown sense of humor. Now, hold on there, Emma, old girl, I told myself, on having sobering second thoughts. You could be wrong, you know. (Lord knows I have been on more than one occasion.) But oh, I hoped not. Not now.

There was, of course, one way to find out. And that meant a trip up to the attic. Well then, so be it. Off I'd go. What could befall me? It was, after all, the middle of the afternoon. This would be no nighttime excursion into the depths of darkness. No supposedly one-armed sea captain would be lying in wait. If I was right, I'd be up and back in no more time than it took Charlie Allbright himself to place it there.

After telling myself all that, why then did I have a feeling of foreboding? It was then the words of warning for my safety from a certain Madame Zerina and those of Sarah Hammond came back to haunt me. For each, in their own way, had spoken of a danger that lay ahead for me. Perhaps, I told myself, I should rethink the whole idea. Might it not, I thought, be more prudent on my part to contact, if not the inspector, then at least the sergeant, with the request that I be accompanied up to the attic? I've no doubt it would have been the wiser move. However, there simply wasn't time. For what if our murderer had come across the gem during last night's midnight walkabout? How then would I appear to the Brighton constabulary?

My plan, as I envisioned it, would be to retrieve the missing gem from where I believed it to be, then set it out in some place where it might more easily be spotted. Having done so, I would see to it that the inspector was informed of my find. I would then put it to him to lie in wait that night within the attic in order to catch 'Captain Hammond' in the act of retrieving it. But before all that could be put in place, I was left on my own to check out my theory as to where I believed the Star of Hyderabad had been hidden on that night a good ten years previous.

And so, with candle in hand, off I went. The creaking of stairs as I made my way up to the attic seemed less menacing than before. As did the attic itself as I entered it. True, it was no less dark but the knowledge of it being afternoon and not the dead of night gave me a certain sense of security. However false that may or may not have been.

In order to make my way over to the object of my search, I once again had to make my way through a storehouse of abandoned, discarded, and forgotten odds and ends of various shapes and sizes. On passing by the old steamer trunk in which Vi and I had found naught but old clothes on that ill-fated night of ours in the attic, I paused and sniffed the air. Most unpleasant, I thought, catching the scent of— what? Whatever it was, it seemed to be emanating from the trunk itself. Another sniff or two. Perfume, I announced to myself. How odd. And cheap perfume at that. The scent?

Nondescript and far too overpowering. *Cheap* perfume, did I say? Oh, no! Good God, I hoped I was wrong in what I was thinking. I shuddered at the thought of having to look inside but knew I must.

The lid I had been careful to re-close when last up here I now saw as being slightly ajar from a bunched-up blanket that hung halfway out of the trunk itself. I very gingerly eased the lid up and threw aside the blanket that lay on top. What I saw was not a pretty picture. There, in a fetal position within the trunk, lay the body of the woman I knew to be Annie Potter—the onetime maid of the Ashcrofts and lady friend to the late Charlie Allbright. A scarf, or rag of some sort, had been twisted round her neck. The face was blue. The lips, dead white. I felt as if I was about to swoon. I closed the lid and rested my hand on the top of it to steady myself.

Would I be next? Alone in a candle-lit attic with a body stuffed in a trunk was not the most enviable position in which to find oneself. My first thought was to hightail it downstairs then and there. In hindsight, it would have been better if I had. But I couldn't leave. Not now. If I was right, the gem was but steps away.

Having regained my composure, at least to a certain degree, I left the trunk and made my way forward until at last coming upon the object of my quest. "We meet again, Madam Mannequin," I announced with a smile, in addressing the alabaster body I now stood before. Needless to say, I received no answer. Although I'd like to think I detected a wisp of a smile. Foolish, I know, but such was the state I was in.

I tipped the candle forward in the direction of the mannequin and, in so doing, it fell from its holder and dropped down into an open box filled with old newspapers. In an instant, flames were shooting up in every direction. I immediately grabbed an old blanket and began to beat the fire out. Those bits of paper still aflame that landed on the floor I stomped on 'til they too were naught but ash. I kicked the box over on its side, retrieved the candle, relit it, and breathed a sigh of relief. My one consolation, other than not having set the place on fire, was that Vi had not been here to witness it all. I could just hear her—"Found the diamond but burned the house down, did you, luv?" Well, I hadn't burned it down and, as yet, I hadn't found the diamond.

This time, being ever so careful, I again moved the candle in closer so that its light fell upon the mannequin's left arm that hung down and slightly away from the body. There on the third finger of the left hand appeared to be a plain band. I reached out and slowly turned it round, right side up. And as I did, there by candlelight shone the Star of Hyderabad in all its magnificence. I very carefully removed it from the finger and, holding it in my hand, turned it this way and that, catching, as I did, the many facets of blue that twinkled as brightly as any star in the heavens. Even then, I could hardly believe I had actually found it. Yet, in retrospect, it should have been obvious. For what better place for such a ring than on a lady's finger? Still, however beautiful it may be (and it was), it was not worth the loss of three lives.

"I'll take the ring now, if you don't mind," whispered a male voice to the back of me. Whispered though it was, the voice was no less menacing in tone. "Pass it here," he said. "But don't look round."

Caught completely by surprise, I actually found myself unable to move. With a heart that had suddenly tripled its beat I remained frozen to the spot, as motionless as the mannequin that stood to the front of me.

"Come on, come on. Hurry it up." The voice, now a growled whisper, was clearly agitated.

After my initial shock, my heart returned to something near its normal beat. I drew in my breath, and slowly exhaled. I realized I'd best get hold of my emotions and the situation I now found myself in if I was to have any chance at all of not winding up alongside Annie Potter. "If this whispering of yours is an attempt to disguise your voice," I said, remaining where I stood with my back to him, "there's really no need to . . . Mr. Christie," I announced dramatically before turning round to face him. As I did, I found myself staring into the barrel of his gun. If I appeared taken aback by the sight of it, Mr. Christie was no less stunned by my having known his identity.

"How'd you know it was me?" he asked, while continuing to brandish the revolver in my face. As unsettling as that was, at least I wasn't subjected to the sight of him in his captain's garb.

"From a number of clues I managed to pick up along the way," I answered, managing as best I could to present an unruffled demeanor to the man. "Not the least," I added, "was a certain fish and chip shop I dropped by earlier this afternoon. From the description I gave of you to its singular employee," I went on, "it seems I was describing old Mr. Christie's grandson. Actually, his 'ne'er-do-well grandson' is the way I believe he described you."

"Ne'er-do-well, am I?" His mouth curled itself into a sneer. "Better that than having to make a living standing over a hot fryer all day like him. 'Nuff of this talk, anyway," he growled. "The diamond—hand it over."

Reluctantly, I obeyed. What else could I do?

"Where'd you find it anyway?" he demanded to know of me.

"Right where Charlie Allbright had placed it—on the mannequin's finger," I announced all too smugly.

"The mannequin!" At that, I was subjected to the most vulgar cursing on his part. As for the mannequin, I thought at one point he was going to kick the poor lifeless thing. "Know how many times I moved that blasted dummy about just to get it out the way?" he ranted. "And all the time—" He shook his head, clearly dumbfounded by the irony of it all.

"Perhaps you might answer a question for me," I said, after he had settled himself down a bit. "How did you know anyone was up in the attic? Or did you?"

"Oh, I knew," he assured me. "I could hear from my room somebody stomping around up here. Thought it might be you. Did a little jig, did you, when you found the diamond, was that it?'' The question was put to me complete with a smarmy little grin.

A little jig? What on earth was he talking about? It was then I realized that what he had heard was my stamping out the flames from the sheets of newspapers that had lain burning on the floor. I let the question pass. I had no intention of relating to him, or to anyone else for that matter, my misadventure with the candle. In any event, it was obvious from the way his eyes never left the diamond that he had little interest in any explanation on my part.

"A beauty, ain't it?" he gloated, holding it up to eye level as he slowly turned it round in his hand. "Could live like a king, I could, a hundred times over from what I'll be able to get for it."

"Because of you," I stated, "there are three people who never got a chance to live even one lifetime."

He eyed me quizzically. "Just how much do you know? Or think you know?" he asked as he pocketed the diamond.

I then proceeded, however foolish it might have been, to enlighten him. "It was you who struck down Dobbs in back of the pub," I announced, rather than posing it as a question. "This after he had sought to bring you into his plan of retrieving the gem from Burbage House."

"And more fool he for having done so, is what I say," he answered, and in so saying, confessing his guilt. "Think I wouldn't have ended up the same way once I'd found it and handed it over to him? It was him or me," he added, "any way you look at it."

"And what of Mr. Latham?" I questioned. "Can you set aside his death so offhandedly as well?"

"It's his own fault for coming up here that night," he stated, as if that in itself justified the man's demise. "Caught me red-handed, you might say. Rummaging about as I was. Don't know who was more surprised, him or me," he added with a chuckle. Evidently, he found it somewhat humorous.

"Dressed as the captain, were you?"

"That's right," he replied. " 'Bloody hell! What's all this then, Christie?' he says on seeing it was me. Well, I knew right away if he ever got back downstairs to tell 'em what he saw, the game would be up then and there."

"So you struck him."

"Lashed out at him," he admitted. "But he moved back, quick-like, and stumbled over something—I don't know what—and down he went. Well, I mean, it wasn't my fault, was it?"

"And you'd have let him live, would you, if he hadn't fallen? I think not," I said in answer to my question.

While I could at last take comfort in having my suspicions confirmed by the man himself, I knew only too well that by admitting his part in it, I stood little, if any, chance at all of him simply letting me walk away. Oh, that Inspector Radcliffe were but hiding in some dark recess of the attic. Ready at a moment's notice from me to spring out and confront him. Since he wasn't, I realized my only option was to keep the man talking in the hope of—what? I didn't quite know. Perhaps Vi or someone might take it in mind to wander up to the attic for whatever reason. Although that was hardly likely, hope springs eternal. "And what reason had you," I asked, plunging right ahead, "for strangling poor Annie Potter? Or should I say Liza Christie? Which name would you prefer?"

After his initial look of surprise, he swung his head in the direction of the trunk then back to me again. "Who told you?" he questioned, with eyes that narrowed in on mine for what seemed the longest time.

"I saw a photo of her in an old newspaper," I answered. "I realized that the woman listed as Ann Potter, maid, was the woman we at Burbage's knew as Liza Christie. She came here with you," I went on, "under the pretense of being your wife—she isn't, is she?" He shook his head no. "Right. The idea," I continued, "being to present to one and all the perfect picture of a couple down from London on their holidays. Wasn't that part of the plan?"

He nodded, adding: "You're smart, you are. Annie said

as much. That was the trouble, see. She got scared after Latham's body was found. We knew you and your lady friend were snooping around trying to find out what's what. Wanted to take off, she did, then and there, and forget about the whole thing.''

"But you, of course, saw things differently. That's why," I added, ''she left a note asking me to meet her at the clock tower. To let me know just what it was that was going on around here."

"That," he informed me, ''was her first and last mistake. Caught her, you see, slipping you that note under your door.''

He then proceeded to tell, for whatever reason and with no prompting on my part, I might add, that he had known the aforementioned Miss Potter back in the days when she'd been working as a maid at Windermere. After having served her time for her part in the robbery and, unable to find work as a maid due to her prison record, she had left Brighton. Evidently, she had no better luck elsewhere. Homesick, she returned to Brighton no more than a year ago with a new profession. Hawking her wares under lamplight was, I believe, how Mr. Christie described it. It was under just such a lamplight that he had chanced upon her. Such was her plight, she was all too eager to take part in his plan for the recovery of the Star of Hyderabad.

"And after all I did for her," he moaned, as if still unable to comprehend it all, ''she tries to queer the plan by tipping you off to it. Soon put a stop to that, I did.''

It was now my turn for a look at the trunk that now served as a coffin for the young woman. "Yes," I said, ''I daresay you did."

"Conscience, that was her trouble," he informed me, as if it were some sort of disease.

"How fortunate for you," I stated testily, ''that you yourself are not afflicted by it.'' He made no reply. I believe my remark passed over his head. Either that or he simply accepted it as fact and thought no more about it one way or the other. As to questioning him in regard to a certain coach and four, I saw no need. It was obvious who the driver had been.

"Sorry, Mrs. Hudson," he spoke at last, leveling his gun at me, "but I've got to look out for myself, haven't I?"

If this was the danger I'd been warned about by Madame Zerina as well as Sarah Hammond, both ladies couldn't have been more on the mark. What to do? What could I do? He raised the revolver, pointed it directly at my head, and clicked back the hammer. Well, don't just stand there, Emma Hudson, I told myself, feeling beads of perspiration upon my brow, do something! Anything! "Don't be a fool," I said, in the hope of reasoning with him. "If you pull that trigger, the sound of the shot will reverberate throughout the entire house." Whether it would or not, I had no idea. Still, I plunged on. "You'll have everyone stampeding up the stairs on the hearing of it. And what then?" I asked. "Do you intend to shoot those who stand in your path? Do you have enough bullets for all? Think again, Mr. Christie." Evidently the picture I painted for him must have had some sort of effect. He lowered the gun while I, in turn, breathed a silent sigh of relief.

"What to do with you then?" he asked, more to himself than to me as he pursed his lips in thought.

"You played the game and lost, Mr. Christie," I stated. "Turn yourself in, man, and take whatever it is that's coming to you."

"Whatever it is that's coming to me?" he repeated with a nasty little chuckle. "Oh, I know only too well what it is that's coming to me if I do." He raised his free hand in a gesture showing himself as being hung. "No, I think not, Mrs. Hudson. Over there!" he barked, pointing to a now all but rungless captain's chair to the left of me. "Sit down and don't move."

I did as I was told. Far better it was than having a bullet put through my head. What now? I wondered. Was I to simply sit there while he made good his escape? Did he really think I would? Obviously not. After rummaging around to the back of me he stepped forward with his find.

A length of rope. I was now quickly and professionally bound to the chair.

"There," he said, on stepping back to admire his hand-iwork, "all nice and secure. And in a captain's chair, at that," he added with a grin. "Fitting somehow, ain't it?"

"And how long am I to remain here?"

He shrugged. "Somebody will be up sooner or later, like as not." Better sooner than later, I thought. "As for me," he stated, "I'm off on the first train bound for London. You can tell Burbage—that is," he added ominously, "if you ever see him again—he can give away what clothes I've left behind in my room. Won't be needing those old threads of mine anymore. Not with this I won't." He grinned and patted the pocketed diamond.

I was then very unceremoniously gagged. But not before I had taken the opportunity to pose a question. "Tell me, Mr. Christie," I asked, "is there actually such a street as Mews Lane?"

"Mews Lane?"

"Yes, you know, it was the street in London where your supposed fish and chip shop was located."

"Oh, that." He shrugged. "Hanged if I know. I've never been to London." And off he went.

So there I sat in the dark, trussed up and unable to move or speak. Any attempt I made on trying to move my arms had the effect of only tightening the rope. Unable to scream or call out for help, the situation seemed hopeless, to say the least. Although my ankles were bound to the staves of the chair, I could manage to move my feet, if only just a little. But perhaps enough to stamp them on the floor as a signal for help. I tried to do so but, with my ankles bound, I could but manage at best a pitiful tap-tap that no one could possibly have heard. Would Vi, in her search for me, ever think to look in the attic? Would I indeed ever be found—alive? And, morbid though it may have been, I found myself wondering just how long it takes for a body to decompose.

TWELVE

Together Again

~~THANKFULLY, I COULD now put aside any idea I had of death or decomposition. For it couldn't have been more than ten minutes, fifteen at the very most, when I heard the sound of feet slowly making their way up the staircase. My heart began to beat excitedly in anticipation of my rescue. But wait! Could it be that for whatever reason, he had decided to return? No, it couldn't have been Christie, for there was a sound of hesitancy to the step. Whoever it was, from my position at the other end of the attic I knew I wouldn't be seen unless someone actually took the trouble to seek me out. Being gagged, the best I could do to be heard was to make odd little grunting noises in my throat. I did so and paused to listen for some sort of reply. Nothing. At least they were still there. I had heard no sound of feet descending the stairs. I again gave forth with a few more throaty grunts. And then, at last—

"Em? Is that you, Em?"

It was Vi! God bless her!

After another combination of gurgles and grunts from yours truly, in she came. I could hear her cautiously making her way through the maze over to me. Wondering all the while, I suspect, just what exactly she'd find.

"'Ere, what's all this?'" she cried out in anguish on coming upon me. "Oh, Em, whatever's happened?" she asked, surveying my trussed-up body. "Are you all right?"

"Mmmm—mmmm," I answered.

"Eh?"

"Mmmm—mmmm," I repeated.

"What? Oh, right. Sorry, luv." She removed the gag from my mouth.

"Thank heaven for that!" I exclaimed with a grateful sigh of relief.

"Who did all this then?" she asked.

"Christie," I answered, wetting my lips. My mouth still had the taste of the rag to it.

"Christie! Christie did this? But—?"

"I'll explain it all later," I said. "Right now, see if you can get me out of this." After much tugging this way and that at the rope, Vi finally admitted she was unable to even so much as loosen it. I suggested she go back downstairs and return with a knife.

"Why, wherever would I get a knife?" she wanted to know.

"From Mr. Burbage—anybody! Only hurry! There may be time yet."

"Time? Time for what?"

"Later, Vi, please," I pleaded. For my only wish now was to be free of my confinement to the chair. Explanations could wait. Off she went, returning minutes later with a huffing, puffing Mr. Burbage, accompanied, to my very great surprise, by none other than Sergeant Styles himself.

"Now you remain calm, Mrs. Hudson," spoke a very nervous and highly agitated Mr. Burbage on seeing me. "Have you free in a jiffy, I will," he added, bringing forth a decidedly wicked-looking knife. If you don't end up stabbing me to death in the process, I thought to myself.

"I'll see to Mrs. Hudson, if you don't mind, Mr. Burbage," said Styles. With the knife now in more competent hands, it took but a few deft strokes before I was at last free. I gave my arms and legs a good rub and rose to a standing position.

"Mrs. Warner tells me that one of the men staying here, a Mr. Christie, is responsible for having tied you up," stated the sergeant. "Is that right?"

"It is indeed," I answered, with yet another rub to my arms.

"Never did like the look of that man," announced Mr. Burbage to no one in particular.

"Why would he do that, Mrs. Hudson?" continued the sergeant. "For what purpose?"

"Sergeant Styles," I replied, "I know you'll need to make a full report on all this, but for now, time is of the essence. Suffice it to say that Mr. Christie now has the Star of Hyderabad in his possession and is at this very moment on his way to, or has already arrived at, the railway station. His destination, London. Now, I suggest—"

"Hold on there, Mrs. Hudson," interjected the sergeant. "You're saying this here Christie bloke has the Star of Hyderabad? The one taken from the Windermere estate? That's a bit much, isn't it? I mean, how can you be sure?"

"Because I gave it to him," I answered.

"You *what?*" he exclaimed.

"Oh, Em, you didn't!" added an equally surprised Violet.

"The Star of Hyderabad?" questioned Mr. Burbage. "Isn't that the diamond Smith, or Allbright, or whatever his name was, was supposed to have stolen? Why, that was a good ten years ago. You remember me telling you about it, don't you, Mrs. Hudson?"

"Yes, Mr. Burbage," I smiled. "I remember."

"Then, if I've got this right," added Styles, "you're saying that you discovered the gem and then, at some point, handed it over to him. But why?"

"Mr. Christie can be quite persuasive, Sergeant. Especially," I added, "when he has a pistol in his hand."

"I see. Yes, of course. And you're saying he's now

headed for the station?'' he asked, to reaffirm my statement.

"If he's not there already," I answered. "What time does the next train leave for London, Mr. Burbage?"

"Six-fifteen, if I'm not mistaken," replied our host.

"And the time now?" I asked. Mr. Burbage brought forth his pocket watch, flipped open the lid, and announced the time as being but one minute to six.

"I suggest, Sergeant," I said, "that you phone the Brighton railway station and have them hold the train until you arrive."

"Hold the train?" He seemed quite taken aback by the idea. "Oh, I dunno—I mean, you're sure, are you, about all this?" I could see the thought of having the train's departure time held up simply on my say-so didn't sit all that well with him. I could see he needed more convincing. "I'd like you to come this way, if you would, Sergeant," I said. And, so saying, set off toward the trunk followed in turn by all three. "More of Mr. Christie's handiwork, I'm afraid," I announced on reopening the lid to reveal its gruesome contents.

"Good God, who's that?" cried the sergeant.

"Why it's Mrs. Christie!" voiced a thoroughly aghast Mr. Burbage.

"There's no need for you to look, Vi," I said. "It's not a pretty sight." But of course she did. And by the look on her face was the worse for having done so.

"He told us she'd left—went back home—family matter," babbled Mr. Burbage to the sergeant. "Mrs. Burbage will be none too pleased by all this, I can tell you."

"Doubt if Mrs. Christie is all that thrilled about it herself," added Vi in a snide aside.

"And you're saying Mr. Christie is responsible for all this, are you?" questioned the sergeant, turning to me.

"He admitted as much," I stated.

He exhaled slowly while pondering, it would seem, all he had heard and seen before at last announcing he'd best call the inspector.

"Yes, of course," I answered. "But first," I urged, "it's

imperative you have the train stopped before it heads out. If it takes off you'll have to call Scotland Yard to have him picked up when it reaches London. "And," I added, "you'll have lost your chance of nabbing him." It didn't take the good sergeant long to realize how the capture would greatly enhance his chances for a position with the Yard.

"Right," he announced. And off we went with the sergeant leading the way back down the stairs.

"A question, Sergeant Styles," I said, as we trooped down the steps. "How is it you're here? Was there something—?"

"Oh, completely forgot, I did." He delved his hand into his pocket and brought forth a folded pamphlet. "Here," he said, handing it over to me. "The street map of London. Had a minute, so I thought I'd pop over here with it."

"Oh," I said, on a note of surprise. "Thank you." After his having made a special trip over with it, I hadn't the nerve to tell him it was no longer needed. Thanks in part to Mr. Christie, I now knew there was no Mews Lane that ran off the Strand in London.

Once downstairs, Mr. Burbage hurried off toward the kitchen, no doubt to inform his wife of this latest disaster in the attic. For his part, Sergeant Styles stepped behind the registration counter to phone. As for Vi and me, we took ourselves into the reading room. Thankfully, it was empty.

As we seated ourselves by the fireplace, Vi was, of course, anxious to hear all the details. I obliged by relating, as I did, my trip to the newspaper office, my finding of the diamond, and my encounter with Mr. Christie. All of which, on the hearing of it, brought forth from my companion expressions of surprise, amazement, and astonishment. And yes, even admonishment for my having gone up to the attic on my own. "Well," I replied with a grateful smile, "as they say, all's well that ends well."

"Not for Mrs. Christie, it didn't," she stated. "Or—what did you say her name really was?"

"Annie," I answered. "Annie Potter."

"Aye, right. Should have made mention of that to the sergeant, Em."

"I intend to," I replied. "Either to him or the inspector at a more convenient time. My one objective upstairs was to get the sergeant to phone the railway station. Hopefully, he has." No sooner had I spoken than he popped his head round the corner for a look-see.

"Ah, there you are, Mrs. Hudson," he smiled. "I thought I saw you come in here. I've just spoken to the stationmaster. He's agreed to hold the train but can't guarantee for how long. I'm on my way over there now with Mr. Burbage. I'll need his help in identifying Christie for me. Oh, and I've spoken to the inspector as well," he added. "He'll be over shortly. You'll be here, will you?"

"I've no intention of going anywhere, Sergeant," I replied.

"Right. Well, I'm off."

"Good luck!" we chorused.

"Now then, Mrs. Warner," said I, turning to my companion, "you speak to me of coming up to the attic alone. How is it you decided to venture up there?"

"That's a story in itself, that is," she answered.

"Well, do get on with it then," I urged.

"To start at the beginning like," she began, "I was sitting 'ere—well, not 'ere, mind, but over there." She motioned to a chair off to one side of us. As to whether where she sat was of any significance to her story, I didn't bother to ask. "Reading the doctor's book, I was," she continued. "And one of his better ones too, I thought. But, after an hour .or so, me eyes started watering, so I set it aside. Thought I'd come up to see how you were getting on. 'Course," she added, in a small measure of annoyance, "I didn't know you had taken off, did I?"

"By that time," I said, "I was probably being bound to a chair, courtesy of Mr. Christie. As for my trip," I questioned, "would you have come on such a day if I had asked?"

"Probably not," she admitted with a grin, before continuing. "So, I opens the door to our room and when I do, no Emma. 'That's queer,' I thought. Then I figured you must be in the loo. But when I checked you weren't there either. On my way back to our room I sees Mr. Christie coming down the hall, right smart-like. ' 'Ere,' I says, 'seen Mrs. Hudson, have you?' 'Yes,' he answers. 'She went out. Said to tell you if I see you, that she wouldn't be back before dark.' "

"He said *that?*" I shook my head in the hearing of it. "Doesn't miss a trick, does he? But what," I asked, "made you think I'd be up in the attic?"

"I'm coming to that," she informed me. " 'There's summat going on around 'ere that's not quite right,' I tells myself. So, back I goes to our room. Once inside, I see your coat draped over the chair. And damp it was. So I knew you'd been out and come back. But where were you, eh? Oh, and right upset I was by this time, thinking 'bout all sorts of things that might have happened to you. And that's when I hears this voice."

"Pardon? What's this you say? You heard a—voice?"

"Aye, that's right," she stated most defensively. "Believe what you like, but it's as true as I'm sitting here."

"I'm not saying I don't believe you, Vi," I hastened to assure her. "Lord only knows, after a week at Burbage's, I'm ready to believe anything. Was it a woman's voice?" I asked, immediately thinking of Sarah.

"No, a man's," she answered.

"A man's! Oh," I said, "could it have been Bert's voice you heard?"

"No, weren't him," she stated. "Well, I'd know me Bert's voice, wouldn't I? No," she said, "it were real posh-like. If you want to know, it sounded to me like—"

"Mr. Latham!" I announced, as a vision of that man's face flashed in my mind.

"Aye," she agreed. "That's what I thought. Broke out in a cold sweat, I did, on hearing it."

"As no doubt would I. But," I questioned, "just what was it he said?"

" 'The attic, Mrs. Warner. Hurry,' " she replied. "Those were his very words."

I was left openmouthed, not knowing quite what to say. No matter. Vi said it all for me. "Looks like you've got yourself a guardian angel in Mr. Latham, Em."

"Yes. At least in this instance it would appear so," I answered, but not before I had offered up to that gentleman, wherever now he might be, a silent prayer of thanks. "So, it was at his urging that you made your way up to the attic—is that what you're saying?" I asked.

"Aye. Well, when you start hearing voices from beyond telling you what to do, it's best to do it, I says. Though I don't mind telling you," she admitted, "that I still wasn't all that keen on the idea."

"But you came. That's the main thing. If you hadn't," I added, with a slight shudder at the thought of it, "I'd probably still be up there."

After the harrowing events of the last few hours we decided to put aside any idea of going in to supper. With memories of the dead woman's body inside the trunk still fresh in our minds, the thought of food didn't sit well with either one of us. In any event, it wasn't long before Inspector Radcliffe put in an appearance.

"I understand you've had quite the time of it today, Mrs. Hudson," spoke the inspector after greetings had been extended by all three parties. "Quite all right now, are you?" he questioned, drawing up a chair and seating himself down between the two of us.

"Yes, quite all right, thank you, Inspector."

"Good. Now then, it appears that congratulations are in order," he announced with a smile. Though I sensed it to be more obligatory than genuine. "That is to say," he went on, "if Styles manages to come back with both that Christie fellow *and* the missing gem. Seems I should have taken you a little more seriously the other day, Mrs. Hudson."

While his smile remained fixed, I couldn't help but feel

it pained him to admit it. I was left with the opinion that while he was relieved the case was all but wrapped up, he would have preferred to have done the wrapping himself. Which, I suppose, was understandable. "Don't blame yourself, Inspector," I said. "I'm afraid when last we spoke I had little to offer up in the way of hard evidence."

"Playing it by ear as we went along. That's what Em and I were doing," spoke Violet.

"Well, whatever your method of operation, it seems to have paid off," he grudgingly admitted. "Now, from what you told me the other day, Mrs. Hudson, and from what little I could learn from Styles over the phone, I have a fair idea of the overall picture. But perhaps you wouldn't mind going over it once again. For the record this time," he added, withdrawing a notepad from his inside pocket.

"Pardon me, Inspector," spoke Vi. " 'Fore you get into all that, shouldn't you be seeing about—" She pointed a finger upwards. "You know—the lady in the trunk."

"Oh, no need to worry yourself about that, Mrs. Warner," he reassured her. "I've already been up there and had my men remove the body before coming in here to see you two."

"Very efficient, I must say," replied Vi.

"Now then, Mrs. Hudson," he said, turning back to me with pencil poised and notebook at the ready, "if you wouldn't mind?"

"Actually, Inspector," I began, while readjusting myself into a more comfortable postion in the chair, "I suppose you could say it all began with the Burbages informing us that what Mrs. Warner had seen in the upstairs hallway, on the first night of our arrival, had been none other than the ghost of Captain Hammond." From there, I continued on with my tale right up to the point in time when I'd been freed by Sergeant Styles from the ropes that had bound me to the chair. That is not to say, however, that the inspector didn't step in from time to time with a question or two of his own. All of which I managed to answer as best I could. Mind, he did seem uncomfortable with the fact that, when in the attic, he had not recognized the body of the woman in the trunk to be that of Annie Potter. I put it to him that it was understandable, since the last time he had seen her would have been during the investigation of the Windermere robbery ten years ago. As for myself, I had had the opportunity of seeing her every day during her stay here at Burbage's. Albeit in the guise of Liza Christie.

"But you had Christie himself pegged right from the start as your number-one suspect, did you?" he asked.

"Oh, my heavens, no, Inspector," I was quick to admit. "No, not in the least."

"Running around in circles, we were," spoke Vi. "Well, I mean," she added defensively, "we had plenty of other suspects, didn't we."

"Perhaps the least being the Burbages themselves," I said. "I had originally thought, Inspector, that Mr. Burbage might have hired someone to pose as the captain. I realized later, he would have had no need. It was, after all, his home. He could have ventured up to the attic at any hour of the night or day and who would have thought anything about it? But sometimes," I confessed, "one becomes so involved in a case that it's . . . how shall I say—?"

"Hard to see the water for the ocean?" offered Vi.

"Yes. Something like that," I smiled. "As for Mr. Trefann being our ghost, Inspector," I continued, "I found it highly unlikely. His story of working in London as a postman had the ring of truth to it. He seemed genuinely proud of having delivered mail to Ten Downing Street. No, he's a Londoner, all right. The man I was looking for would have had to be from Brighton itself. Someone whom Dobbs would have known. Although Mr. Trefann's absence at one point—due, we were told, to some such ailment or other—gave me pause to wonder. And then," I added, "there was that business with the wedding ring."

"Wedding ring?" he asked. "What wedding ring was that?"

I answered that it was my belief, which later turned out to be true, that the murderer, on checking in, had brought along a female accomplice in order to pose as a couple down from London on holiday. "On my noting that Mrs. Trefann possessed no wedding ring," I added, "my suspicions, for a time, shifted to them."

He nodded understandingly. "A false lead. Yes, they can, as Mrs. Warner says, run you around in circles sometimes. But what about this Peter Jones you mentioned earlier?" he asked.

"Aye. He's the one I had me money on," admitted Vi.

"True, we did find him bending over the body of Mr. Latham when coming upon him in the attic," I said. "But, knowing of his belief in spiritual visitations from the beyond, his story of believing Latham's death was caused by his having a heart attack when confronted by the captain was presented as a plausible explanation. One that he offered up in a honest and straightforward manner. At best a guileless young man."

"Aye. But he was too quiet for my liking," added Vi. "Always kept to himself, like. And what about the letter, eh?"

"Letter?" questioned Radcliffe. "What letter is this?"

"I was informed by Mr. Jones, Inspector, that he had mailed off a letter to his wife. To ask that she come down. It seems he had had some sort of lovers' quarrel with her prior to leaving London. The letter was a request that she take the next train to Brighton."

"But there was no letter actually sent? Is that what you're saying?"

"Quite. Which led me to speculate as to whether indeed there was a wife. And whether all that he had told me was true." I then made a mental note that before returning home, I would confront our Mr. Jones for an explanation. "But be that as it may," I continued, "I found Mr. Christie's actions to be the more suspicious of the two."

"How's that?"

"According to Mr. Christie," I said, "it was supposed to have been the first trip down to Brighton for him and his . . . shall we say 'wife'? Yet they spoke quite knowledgeably to Mrs. Warner and me of what sights there were to be seen here. And his story of seeing the ghost of Captain Hammond was, unlike Mr. Trefann's, highly imaginative, to say the least. At one point, he spoke of seeing the captain extend his arm upwards and float to the ceiling. In doing so, he pantomimed the action by extending his right arm upwards. But," I added, "it was the right arm the captain was missing. He made the same mistake when he tucked the left sleeve into the captain's coat when masquerading as Hammond. While I realized this could hardly be construed as solid evidence, it was enough for me to be more than a little suspicious of him. As I had discounted his story of seeing Captain Hammond as being the reason for the two of them not leaving their room on the night of Latham's death," I continued, "I was left to wonder why it was they had chosen not to put in an appearance. When one is left with unanswered questions, one tends to become suspicious. From what we now know, it would appear that Christie was afraid the woman might be recognized by the police. Having, no doubt, been picked up or told to move along a number of times in connection with, shall we say, her nighttime profession."

"Then," queried the inspector, "the turning point, when you knew it was Christie, came when—?"

"When I saw the photo of Liza Christie or—the woman we now know was Annie Potter—in the newspaper. I followed that up with a return trip to the fish and chip shop. There I found that Christie was the grandson of the man who owned it. And that Christie himself lived in a room in back of it."

"Very nicely done, Mrs. Hudson," he acknowledged with a smile. "Again, my congratulations." This time I believed he meant it. "Now," he said, "all we need is to hear from Styles that—"

"Oh, Inspector." We looked up to see Mrs. Burbage standing in the doorway. "The telephone," she said. "It's for you."

"Speak of the devil!" he exclaimed, before rising from

his chair and heading off at a good clip out of the room.

Mrs. Burbage, who had remained standing in the doorway, advanced toward us bearing a pained expression. "Oh, Mrs. Hudson," said she, "I was ever so shocked and sorry to hear from Mr. Burbage 'fore he left what had happened to you. You're all right now, are you?" I answered that I was. "Oh, it's terrible. Just terrible," she moaned. "The things that have been going on around here—well, I just don't know what to make of it all. Sell, yes, that's what I'll do," she announced to the two of us. "I'll have Mr. Burbage look into it first thing in the morning, I will. The sooner we leave, the better." Vi quizzed her as to what Mr. Burbage would think about the idea of selling. "It's not a question of what Mr. Burbage thinks," she retorted. "I'll not stay here a minute longer than I have to. You ladies are fortunate to be leaving tomorrow."

"Aye, if we can make it through another night, that is," was my companion's caustic comment.

"I can well understand your attitude, Mrs. Warner," stated the woman. "Which brings me to the other reason I had for wanting to speak to Mrs. Hudson as well as yourself. When you hand in your keys tomorrow morning," she continued, "there'll be a check waiting for the both of you."

"A check?" I repeated. "I don't understand."

"The money you ladies put out for your lodgings," she informed us, "will be returned to you. It's the least I can do."

Vi and I were caught completely by surprise. "I won't say it won't be appreciated," I replied, after an offering up of thank you's.

"Yes, well," she said, appearing somewhat flustered and embarrassed by this singular act of generosity on her part, "I . . . ah . . . I'd best be off then. And let me know," she added, before making her exit, "if there's anything you need. Tea, perhaps?"

"Tea? Yes; that would be lovely," I answered. "We'll take it in the dining room in a few minutes. Well," said I, turning to Vi on once more finding ourselves alone, "a check—I certainly didn't expect that." Violet's response was that we should take the check and go on a holiday. My laughter at her remark was cut short by Inspector Radcliffe reentering the room, beaming from ear to ear.

"That was Styles," he announced. "He's nabbed Christie. *And* the diamond!" he added with a gleeful rubbing of hands.

After congratulations had been extended all round, we were informed by the inspector that we'd be required back in Brighton to testify at the trial once it had actually come before the courts. I stated he had but to let us know the date. Vi's added comment was that when next we came to Brighton he could be ruddy well sure we wouldn't be staying at Burbage House. And on that, Inspector Radcliffe took his leave and we took our tea. Then it was back upstairs where we were later to enjoy the best night's sleep that we had had since our arrival.

Morning found us downstairs, packed and ready to leave. It was Mr. Burbage himself, all puffed up with importance on having been in on the capture of Christie, who handed the check over to us. After dutifully thanking him, I made mention of the fact that Mrs. Burbage was of a mind to sell the establishment.

"Humph!" he snorted. "Over my dead body, she will."

" 'Ere," said Vi, "best be careful what you say 'bout dead bodies and all. Especially round 'ere."

"What? Oh, yes, I see what you mean," he answered with a good-natured laugh.

"Ah, Mrs. Hudson, there you are."

I turned round to see Mr. Jones enter through the front door, accompanied by a very pretty young woman on his arm.

"Here she is," he announced with a smile on crossing over to us. "My Cathie. She's come, you see."

"Well, this is a surprise," I said. Which indeed it was. Vi and I were quite taken with the woman who appeared somewhat demure if not a little shy on finding herself the center of our attention.

"I owe it all to you, Mrs. Hudson," he stated. "If you hadn't got after me to write—"

"Write? But Mr. Jones," was my perplexed reply, "I was under the impression you had sent no letter."

"Letter? Oh," he said, "no, it wasn't a letter I sent. It was a telegram, see. Get there quicker, it would, I figured."

"A telegram?" I looked at Vi. She looked at me. What could I say? What I did say, before he hurried off to sign his wife in, was to wish them both a pleasant stay.

"Got everything then, have you, luv?" asked Vi. "Don't want to be leaving anything behind."

"Yes, I believe so," I answered. "Oh, no," I suddenly announced with a groan on remembering. "That sachet you gave me. I don't remember packing it. It must still be in the dresser drawer."

"Best forget about it then," she advised. "No need to go all the way back up just to get it."

"Forget about it? I should say not!" I stated. Knowing, for all that she said, if I didn't, I'd never hear the last of it. "It won't take a minute," I added, before once again (and hopefully for the last time) heading up the stairs and back down the hall to our room.

On entering, the first thing I noticed was the chill in the air. The next thing I noticed was the apparition of Sarah Hammond. She stood at the end of the room with her back to me, gazing out the window. I quietly closed the door behind me but held onto the doorknob for support. My legs were wobbly and my breathing slightly labored. "Mrs. Hammond," I called out softly to get her attention. Though I've no doubt she was aware of my presence. Why I called out or what I intended to say, I hadn't the foggiest. Yet I couldn't just stand there.

"There's much to be done," she said. Whether to me or to herself, I had no idea. "The garden's overgrown with weeds. John should be here to see to it," she added, turning to face me.

"But your husband's not here anymore, Mrs. Hammond," I said with my pity for her overriding any sense of fear I felt. "He's gone, Mrs. Hammond. Go to him," I said. "Your time here is over." I believe I had at last gotten through to her. For she looked at me in a most quizzical way.

"Gone?" she said. "John's not here?"

"He awaits you on the other side," I answered. "Out there."

She turned from me to once more face the window. It was a stance she continued for what seemed the longest time. "Yes," she suddenly announced, breaking the stillness of the room. "I see him! I see him!" Her voice, previously a dull monotone, was now filled with heartrending emotion. "He beckons," she sang out. "He beckons to me!"

"Then go to him, Mrs. Hammond," I urged. "Now, while you have this moment in time."

She stretched out her arms in a gesture of open embrace. "John," she cried out. I, of course, was not privy to the sight of her husband that only she could now see. And, on advancing forward, Sarah Hammond stepped into eternity. To be seen no more by the eyes of mortal man.

"Found it then, did you?" asked Vi on my return.

"Found it? Found what?"

"Why, the sachet, of course!" she replied in annoyance.

"Oh, yes, the sachet," I mumbled. "Yes," I lied. "I found it in the drawer where I'd left it. I've put it in my purse." I hadn't found it, of course. I had completely forgotten about it. Understandable though, wouldn't you say?

Once outside and with our luggage piled aboard the carriage, we climbed inside and settled ourselves down.

"Well, like you say, Em," announced Violet, "all's well that ends well."

"Yes," I answered. "And not just for us. Sergeant Styles's capture of Christie and his recovery of the diamond from him should sit well with Inspector Lestrade. If the good sergeant intends to go ahead with his application to the Yard.''

"Aye. And don't forget Mr. Burbage. Seemed quite pleased with himself for having taken a part in it all. And,'' she added, ''what about the Joneses, eh? Nice to know they're back together again, ain't it?''

"Back together again,'' I repeated softly to myself. And, as the carriage began to pull away, I gave one last look up to the window of our room where Sarah Hammond had stood but minutes before. ''Yes,'' I said, ''isn't it.''